THE DETERMINED BRIDE

COBBLE CREEK SMALL TOWN ROMANCE
(PREVIOUSLY PUBLISHES AS THE SNAPSHOT BRIDE)

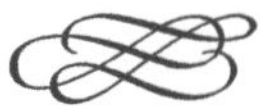

KIMBERLY KREY

Candle
House
Publishing

THE DETERMINED BRIDE: Cobble Creek Small Town Romance

This title was previously published as The Snapshot Bride

❀ Created with Vellum

CHAPTER 1

Kira stared at the bronze casket, an arrangement of yellow roses and lush green leaves draped over the top.

"Would you like to say a few words about Papa Moretti before they start the closing hymn? This is your last chance." Mom's voice had come out urgent and pleading. Maybe she really *did* know how much he meant to Kira. At least someone did.

"I think so," Kira said with a nod. Moments before, Dad had delivered a flawless retelling of Angelo Moretti's life at a glance. Marissa, Kira's poised-even-in-mourning sister, talked of her admiration of his many accomplishments. His pastor was next. When they opened remarks to the congregation, a few of his neighbors walked up to the podium to speak of what a great man he was. They were heartfelt comments, and all of them were true, but Kira had something of her own to share.

Something that—in her mind—set this beautiful soul apart from the rest of the world.

She gulped hard, steadied herself with a grip on the pew, and shuffled around the row of stocking-covered knees. A potpourri of perfumes wafted from the row where Papa's sisters sat, dabbing at their faces with gnarled tissues. Seven long strides took Kira to the pulpit. She wobbled just once, which was good considering the size of her heels.

Kira licked her lips and cleared the tears from her throat with a forced cough. "Um … so I'm not going to sound as eloquent as everyone else," she admitted with a shrug. "But in my defense, I've never taken a public speaking class the way Marissa has. Aunt Tullie claims she hasn't taken a class either, but I can't help but think she's lying after that prayer, because … that was something else."

The faces in the crowd were blank and lifeless, like paper dolls. Mom pulled the net of her black funeral hat over her eyes. Dad put his head down. Kira knew what he was thinking: *Why can't Kira just stay in the shadows? As unintentional as it may have been, Kira has muddied the Moretti name. Why insist on showing her face?*

She dropped her gaze to the wood grain of the pulpit, running her thumb along the edge as she continued. "No one had a sense of humor like Papa Moretti. Some of you mentioned that already. He used to say to me, *Hey kid, when you going to grow already? I swear each time I see you ya shrink.*"

Two distinct courtesy laughs floated over the pews. A fresh sweat broke across Kira's brow. "But really," Kira continued, "the best thing about him was that he had a way of making everyone feel special. No, not special. It's …" Heat filled her face. She knew there was a better word. She could picture Grandpa saying it now as they sat at the diner across from his studio, dipping hot fries into creamy milkshakes.

"*Exceptional*—that's what I was looking for. He had a way of seeing the best in everyone, even the screw-ups. I ought to know. But I think that's what made him such a great photographer, you know? He looked at someone, and he could *see* their real beauty. It's one of the first things he taught me when I got my camera. During the time I spent with him at his studio, I watched him direct people with such precision. A slight tip of the head. Lift of the chin …"

Kira lost that thought as the piano player, who worked for the funeral home, crept slowly toward the piano in her sweater dress and winter boots—boots that let out a whistle as they scuffed each other in stride.

"Oh, looks like they're *cuing the music*." She shot the piano player a teasing grin, but the woman didn't look up to catch it. "I know Grandpa saw good things in me, too. He told me all the time, but I could see it in his face, too. The way he looked at me, like he actually admired me." She gulped hard once more and turned to the box where he lay. "Papa, I never did anything to earn that admiration. I never gave you a reason to call me exceptional, but I promise that someday I will."

Kira's promise stuck with her while she mouthed the hymn, her voice too raspy to actually sing aloud. At the graveside service, as she peeked into the six-foot hole beneath the suspended casket, that promise began to haunt her. She wanted nothing more than to finally become worthy of Papa Moretti's faith. But she'd wanted to do that while he was alive. It just hadn't worked. Deep down, he had to secretly agree with the family consensus: Kira was flighty, flaky, and was too distracted to stick with a task long enough to succeed at it. Still, even if her grandfather *did* agree, there was one distinct difference in his perception: while Kira's family was convinced that things would never change, Papa Moretti had remained positive that she could—and would—surprise them all.

A soft burning swelled in her heart. Not a mean heat, just a gentle warmth that assured her she could do that very thing.

Please ... show me how I can keep that promise. Show me how I can prove them wrong, and prove you right.

Kira sat in a daze, eyes open wide but not seeing at all. And she wasn't the only one stunned. Whispers rose from behind.

"You've *got* to be kidding," Marissa mumbled.

"Yes, there has to be some sort of mistake." Aunt Mable sounded baffled.

"It's not a mistake," Marissa assured, her hushed voice thick with irritation. "Kira's the only one who doesn't have a life. No one else could up and leave everything behind."

"Excuse me," the portly, red-faced executor said. The man, who insisted on being called *Mr. Executor,* wore a sweater with a white collared shirt beneath and a sports coat on top of it all. Must not be from Nevada.

Gramps's lawyer, Mr. Holden, who sat next to the man at the desk, nudged a pair of gold-rimmed glasses up the bridge of his nose with a clenched fist. "Angelo insisted on this formal reading because he wanted to *avoid* a family dispute. Please listen to the stipulations accompanying the studio and duplex, as it might answer some of your questions."

Kira lifted her shoulders. Somewhere along the way they'd started to droop.

Mr. Executor ran a pointed finger over the page. "Let's see … where was I? *Ah*—Starting back at the top of *paragraph twenty-four, page six*: 'I leave Studio Click, the photography studio at 726 Main, Cobble Creek, Wyoming, to my granddaughter, Kira Moretti, as well as the duplex on 375 Chapel Street. Kira is the only family member who's expressed a desire to live in Cobble Creek and run the studio. In addition, Kira has shown a natural interest and talent for the craft from a young age, which she amply demonstrated during her recent preliminary stay.'"

The Executor peeked up to meet Kira's gaze, proving he knew who she was. Mr. Holden did the same before turning a scrutinizing gaze to the others, seeming to challenge them: *speak now or hold your peace for good.* Packed among her aunts and great-aunts, each donning their Sunday best, Kira stayed silent, hoping they couldn't detect the enormous knot of regret building within her. f time machines existed, Kira would score one for herself and set it back to the *preliminary stay* Gramps referred to in his statement.

The two men dropped their gaze back to the legal-sized stack of papers.

"It goes on as follows," the executor said. "'I've lived a frugal life, saved up my retirement funds, and pursued something I loved even more than financing, imagine that. I've left you all equal shares—all but Kira. But if for any reason she chooses *not* to take over the studio *and* live in and manage the duplex in Cobble Creek, both properties are to be sold to the highest bidder. Kira will take a cut equal to the thirteen thousand dollars the other family members received and any further profits will be split between the church at the address stated below and the National Cancer Foundation.'"

The hush had died down long ago. It remained quiet as Mr. Holden pinched the wire rim of his glasses and wiggled them off his face. "I'm sure you all understand the reason he chose to do it this way, but if you don't, I'll spell it out for you." His narrow face turned severe, the sharp angles looking angry as he glared over the nervous huddle. "He didn't want you harassing Ms. Kira or waiting for her to fail so you could all take a bigger cut. He was too nice to come out and say it, even to me, but that was his concern." He looked from one face to the next before nodding toward the stack on the desk once more. "We've got a few more things to take care of, and then you're all free to leave."

Thoughts of a whole new life poured into Kira's mind. It was like the time she'd fallen asleep in her bed and woken up to find her parents had packed her and Marissa into the minivan at night. They'd driven all the way to Magic Land, a theme park she and her sister had been dreaming about since they could speak.

Kira hadn't known it was coming, and she was definitely excited about it, but a hint of fear lingered among the thrill. Back then, Kira was scared of the *Coaster Kong*. Here, among the hushed, doubting tones of her family, the fear was obvious: failure.

But this time, Kira wouldn't disappoint. With the opportunity before her, Kira's prayer circled through her mind once more. *Help me prove that Papa Moretti was right to trust me. Help me to clear the Moretti name.*

CHAPTER 2

Anthony stared down at the check, bright beneath the lamplight's glow, and wiped a tear from his face. Thirteen thousand dollars. That was a whole lot of money to leave a guy who wasn't even family. He wondered how much the man had left those who *were* family.

At the thought, a vision of Kira Moretti came to mind. Dang, she'd grown into those big brown eyes. If he'd have worked up the nerve to say hello at the funeral, would the brunette have remembered him? Probably not. It'd been years since he'd seen her stroll into the diner with her granddad.

Anthony had always looked forward to seeing the cute girl each summer. The two would often sneak off and get into some sort of mischief. Chasing frogs along the grassy trail. Collecting grasshoppers and caterpillars in jars. Of course, one of those visits was more memorable than the rest. What were they, ten—no—eleven. Still, he hadn't forgotten. How could he? It was his first kiss.

A spark lit up low in his belly as he recalled the way she'd taken hold of his hand, dragged him across the back alley and toward Lakeview Park.

"Throw in a rock and you'll get a wish," she told him. Anthony knew he'd catch the wrath from his dad for leaving, but it was hard to say no to someone like Kira. Spunky, carefree, and unafraid of consequences. That's what made her stand out most—he'd known plenty of kids who didn't think twice about what punishment might come their way. But they were operating under ignorance. Kira, on the other hand, knew dang well what would happen if she snuck off without telling her parents; she'd told him as much on their way back to the diner.

"My dad's going to kill me," she said with a grin. "He gets furious when I run off without telling anyone."

"So why do you do it?" he couldn't help but ask.

She shrugged, then pushed the black wisps of her hair from her face. "Why not? They already know I'm going to. Marissa's the obedient one. Not me."

It stood out to him, even then, that she seemed to "know her place." She'd been labeled, and she planned to live up to it. As an only child, Anthony never knew what it was like to be compared to a sibling. But the idea of having someone to measure up to … he could see how that could play tricks on a kid's head.

She'd owned a soft spot in his heart ever since. He wanted to know how much she'd changed over the years. He wanted to know if he'd ever see her again. But more than that, he wanted to smack himself upside the head for not approaching her at the funeral, to offer his condolences at least. But leave it to Kira to be the only one *not* standing beside the casket to receive people. Off doing her own thing. Perhaps she hadn't changed much after all.

In a blink, he was back at the water's edge. Preparing to toss in his rock.

"Get it past the row of cattail and you get a wish."

Anthony gave her a look. "Who says?"

Kira shrugged. "Everyone."

He palmed the soft, gray stone in his hand. It was heavy and nearly as big as his fist. He should've picked a smaller one, but it was too late now. With a determined breath, eyes focused on the cattail swaying in the sunlight, he reared his arm back and hurled the stone toward the glistening water.

The pale gray orb spun as it soared up and barely beyond the tall, golden plants. It hit a dry sprig of one, even, before plopping into the pond.

"You did it!" She jumped in place twice before taking a hold of his shirt with her fists and pulling him close. At once, her lips were on his.

Anthony froze. Waiting for his body to catch up with the realization. Kiss her back, *his mind pled, but she pulled back before he could.*

She patted his shoulder. "You get a kiss if you hit one of the cattails. I forgot to tell you that part."

Anthony nodded. "So I still get a wish?"

"Yep," she said with a grin.

"What if my wish is to get another kiss?"

Kira shrugged. "I guess we'll have to see if it comes true. Come on." She grabbed his hand once more. "We better get back."

Anthony sank deeper into his office chair, the old wheels squeaking beneath the shift in weight. Cracks along both armrests threatened to pinch his skin if he forgot himself, which he did daily. He glanced down at the check on the desk once more. Anthony would put Angelo Moretti's money to use just how he'd taught him. *"Make your money earn money; it's the way of the wise man."* Anthony had already put that into practice. Still, before he invested Angelo's gifted sum, Anthony *would* allow himself one luxury, he decided, as the seat let out another groan. Something he'd been denying himself for a very long time: a new office chair.

He hadn't meant to let it happen, but Anthony's mind drifted back to the funeral, Kira standing behind the pulpit, her wide eyes rimmed in red. For a woman as proud as she seemed to be, she'd appeared vulnerable in that moment. Even in recollection, the sincerity of her words struck a spot inside Anthony. That undying drive to be good enough. The desperation to prove yourself worthy in someone else's eyes. He related to that. But the woman he'd tried to impress—or gain the attention of, at least—had abandoned him long, long ago. If only the hope for her return could've vanished so quickly.

While giving in to a yawn, Anthony captured the gold pull chain on his desk lamp between two fingers and gave it a tug. He hunkered into the worn seat as darkness took over. He missed Dad. Attending Mr. Moretti's funeral had brought back some of the pain. Probably because the kind old man had treated him like a son—or *grand*son, was more like it.

He thought back on the day after Dad's burial, when he'd stepped into the diner to prep for the day. Angelo showed up just a few minutes after he'd unlocked the place and flicked the lights on. At first Anthony thought he was there for an early cup of coffee or maybe to grab a stack of hotcakes before the place officially opened. But the old man surprised him by strapping on an apron, washing up, and asking how he could help. *How*—not if.

His presence had been such a welcome kindness that Anthony hadn't been able to say no. It wasn't that he couldn't prep the diner on his own; he'd done that for years, and Angelo knew it. But his father had always been sitting in that corner booth, a mug of coffee at his side, going over numbers with a stack of receipts and his printable calculator. A task Anthony had since moved to the close of each day, rather than the beginning; he liked going to bed knowing where he stood. How much his employees made in tips. How much overhead he had to work with. Business had been good to him. But even still, he would forever miss the sound of Dad tapping out numbers from the corner booth in the early morning light.

Anthony shuffled out of his office, keying in on the spot of light glowing from above the kitchen sink. Thank heavens winter was on its way out. As much as he enjoyed the snow, the cozy comfort of a warm fire on a winter's night, Anthony wasn't a fan of the shortened hours of daylight. Or the darkness that reached well into the morning and arrived way too soon each day. An uninvited guest who came and went as it pleased. He poured himself a tall glass of milk and tipped it back as his mind drifted to a different sort of guest: the brown-eyed girl who'd caught his attention once more. The chances of him seeing her again were slim now that Angelo had passed, which meant he may just have to take action himself. Whether he had to get on social media or ask Gordon for the man's emergency contact numbers, Anthony knew he should try and see Kira Moretti again.

CHAPTER 3

The duplex Kira inherited on Chapel Street was cozy, clean, and charming. It offered mirror images of the exact same layout, side by side. Each consisted of a small kitchen and dining area, a modest-sized front room, two bedrooms, and one bath—her favorite part being the claw-foot tub and pedestal sink. It was delightful. And though Kira had only moved in the day before, she was already enjoying her favorite thing about the place—the large windows.

Generous amounts of morning sun poured into the kitchen from the east, illuminating the bright cabinets and natural wood with its heavenly glow. In the afternoon before the sun set, its rich brilliance seeped into every visible nook of the front room, drenching it with vibrant color and warmth. But best of all, the duplex reminded Kira of her beloved Papa. The little nook by the window where he'd read to her before bed. The hallway he'd lumbered down with a paper bag over his head while growling like a monster. And then more recent memories when she came to shadow him at the studio. Sitting at the quaint little breakfast nook, chatting over a mug of coffee.

In the week following his funeral, Papa's sisters had cleared out his clothing and personal items before hiring a cleaning crew to finish up. She'd been grateful to see that—along with the furnishings and linens—they'd left familiar blankets she remembered curling up in by the gas fireplace. And the lacy curtains that reminded her of Grandma.

Kira shook her head. She could hardly believe he'd really left the place to her. His *Kira Kira* and no one else. Her mind drifted back to the moment the will was read. Marissa had implied that Kira could only take over because she didn't have a life to leave behind. That might not have been a fair statement—considering that Kira had a job, an apartment, and a handful of close friends—but truthfully, Kira hadn't been living a life she would miss a whole lot. She felt more as if she were in limbo. That she'd been waiting for her *real life* to start. Perhaps now it could.

She dumped a fresh load of laundry onto the massive wool rug by the window and plopped down beside it. With her back strategically to the morning sun, Kira soaked up the heat as she folded towels and washcloths. She'd poured in a generous amount of Downey, a scent that reminded her of pairing socks and folding towels with Grandma before she passed.

God, thanks for giving me those memories. Thanks for giving me this chance. Help me not to mess it up ... The words "like I do everything else" trailed off in her mind. No, she refused to drag her past around the quaint town of Cobble Creek. Today was a new day, and she could hardly wait to explore it.

With the calming sound of Beethoven's Moonlight Sonata

drifting through the kitchen, she stacked the freshly folded linens into the wicker basket and proceeded to make a numbered to-do list. As a collector of notepads, Kira had dozens to choose from. Today's featured a cartoon drawing of a businesswoman in a skirt suit with red heels and a matching purse. Instead of the usual "to-do list" topping each sheet, this notepad read: "Things I'll Tackle Today." It felt appropriate, considering her new venture.

1. *Introduce myself to the tenants next door.* She was their new landlord, after all. Weird—she couldn't imagine herself fitting the part.

2. *Check out the studio.* Kira needed to see what Papa had in the way of backdrops and props and see what she'd like to add to the collection to make it more of her own.

3. *Find volunteers to take studio test shots.* It had been a while, after all. She couldn't remember the last time she'd pulled out her camera and she'd need a quick refresh on settings and make sure her flash would sync to the lights in the studio.

3. *Buy coffee. Immediately. And groceries.*

4. *Get business booming before Marissa visits in May.*

The last item on her list would get transferred to each subsequent list Kira made out as the days passed by, seeing that it was close to three months away. But she needed to stay focused. And impressing her sister—proving to her family that she could be successful here in Cobble Creek—would be all the incentive she'd need. After the reading of Papa's will, Mom, Dad, and Marissa put on happy faces. They'd even mustered a few strangled words of encouragement. But the fear on their faces was as undeniable as it was legible: *Why would Papa Moretti set Kira up for a failure so big?*

But she wouldn't fail. She refused to.

With the list tucked into her purse, Kira wedged her feet into a pair of black leather pumps. She'd settled on the same type of outfit she'd worn while shooting runway photos: skinny black pants and a matching blazer over a white, lacy camisole. The shoes, of course, would offer the same sort of sophistication. Not too high or flashy. Practical, but elegant. Her mom might call them classy, but since the woman had abused the term on so many levels, Kira had cut it out of her vocabulary completely.

As she locked the front door, Kira caught sight of an old sedan parked out front of the unit beside hers. According to the lease, the tenant was a single mom with an eight-year-old boy. Kira swept a hand over her slicked-back hair and repositioned her backpack purse over one shoulder. Maybe the woman and her boy were sleeping in. It was Saturday, after all. Better to wait and introduce herself when she got back.

Kira strutted toward her red, compact car instead, eyes widening as she noticed something she hadn't expected. "Ice? In March?" Wasn't all of that supposed to go away after Christmas or Valentine's Day? Sure, she'd noticed the cold air on her face and fingers, but this was proof that winter—at least in Cobble Creek—was hanging on for dear life. She cringed, her footsteps slowing as she took in the thick layer of frost coating the windshield. Seemed impossible with the sun shining so brightly. Of course, this side of the duplex wouldn't see the sun until later. This was definitely different from Vegas. No worries. She'd warm up the car, let the wipers scrape off the frost, and tackle the other items on her list.

❧

Anthony wiped down the countertop, eyes drifting over the faces in the booths. The folks of Cobble Creek had called Tony's Diner home for a whole lot of years. It felt like family, and he was grateful to be a part of it. Usually the patrons were fairly diverse where age was concerned, but it seemed as if he'd posted a sign out front his window that morning: *newlyweds only. Hand-holding, food-sharing, and flirting required.* It wasn't that he minded being surrounded by the happy couples. Heck, the recent chain of back-to-back marriages in Cobble Creek had given him hope. Women really were still vowing to spend their lives with someone. Seeking a loving, devoted union. They just weren't looking to make those vows with him.

He dropped the washcloth into the bleach bin and leaned his back against the counter. Tables five, seven, and nine held three of Cobble Creek's newest couples. Bear and Maddie Schaefer sat with their new little addition bundled in a carrying seat that was covered by a blanket sporting black bears and forest trees. Frankie and Logan sat at the next table, their school-aged girl, Harper, toying with the whipped cream on her waffles as she giggled over something Logan said. The man had been through it over the years, but it seemed time had dealt him a hand that forced those hardships back to their rightful place: the past. How would it be to have life changed so suddenly—into something as wonderful as the life he'd found, that is?

If Anthony really wanted to know the answer to that, he

could try asking Sheriff Lockheart. AKA the guy who married the gal Anthony had had a mini-crush on for a solid year before Trent Lockheart came into the picture. Not that he'd done a whole lot about it. Sure, he'd asked Jessie on a date a time or two, but they'd never gone out. He guessed that was probably a good thing, seeing that she was happily married now, just like the lucky row along the south side of the diner. Anthony didn't exactly feel like he should be married already—heck, twenty-seven was still plenty young. But he couldn't help but wonder how he would ever meet that special lady. The one just for him.

"... would love it if she'd come model for a free session. What do you think?" Anthony was almost positive he'd heard that voice recently. The warm, even tone—tinged with hints of an Italian Brooklyn accent—made him wonder if he were hearing things; he had yet to meet a woman in Cobble Creek who had an accent so similar to his. But as Anthony leaned around Gordon, the man sipping back a late-morning cup of coffee, he spotted her—Kira Moretti.

Anthony froze in place, feeling like his insides had been tossed into a food processor.

Dressed in black from bottom to top, a wide smile on her heart-shaped face, Kira squatted beside the Wells family.

"Can I?" he heard Harper ask, her eyes lit up like Easter had come early.

"I guess a few pictures wouldn't hurt," Logan said.

Harper broke into a celebration dance.

"Perfect." Kira straightened up. "Bring her on over once you're finished and we'll ..." She stopped talking, and for a moment, Anthony wasn't sure why. But then it struck him—she was looking at him. Did she remember him from all those years ago?

He thought she'd looked beautiful when he'd seen her a few weeks back, but she looked stunning now. Flushed cheeks, dark lashes, and a smile that could make a guy's legs wobblier than a newborn colt's.

"I, um …" She stuttered, looking back at the small family. "We'll see you across the street once you're finished."

"Sounds great," Frankie said.

Harper rubbed her palms together. "I can't wait."

Anthony straightened up as—without so much as another word—Kira strode toward him. The corner of her full lips quirked up on one side. "I know you," she breathed, her eyes narrowing in concentration.

His heart sputtered and clanked. "You do?"

"Don't you remember me?" She draped a slender arm along the bar. "I'm Angelo's granddaughter, Kira."

Anthony shook his head. "No. I mean, yes. Of course I remember. I just wasn't sure *you* would."

She nodded slowly as the smile widened and then leaned toward him, her shoulders hunching as she neared. "You were my first kiss," she said in a hush. "How could I forget?"

It felt like Anthony had just pulled the lid off a stockpot. Heat filled his face. Perhaps his brain was simmering somewhere in the stock, because he couldn't exactly find it in the moment of shock.

"Sorry," Kira said, looking anything but. "Did I embarrass you?"

Anthony grabbed a handful of apron and shirt at his chest,

gave it a few tugs to get some air. "No," he lied. "I don't … are you kiddin'? Takes a lot to embarrass *this* guy."

She giggled, and he'd be danged if he didn't feel it all the way to his toes. Her eyes shot to his hand, the left hand resting on the counter, before looking back to him. "You know my grandpa passed, right?"

"Of course. I was at his funeral."

Kira ducked her head, her persona shifting in a blink. "Uh, so you heard me rambling up there like an idiot?" She glanced over her shoulder to where Harper and her family finished their brunch, then dragged a stool out and climbed up. "I really shouldn't do stuff like that."

"Like what?" Anthony asked. "Lighten things up? Tell folks what he was like from *your* perspective—which happens to be similar to mine."

Kira's gaze shot from her folded hands to his face.

"You were perfect," he said with a nod. "Trust me." He studied her face, watched as she shed at least of few of the insecurities that had crept in.

"Thanks."

It wasn't an uncommon word by any means. Heck, Anthony probably heard and said it himself more times than he could count in a day. But there was something about the sincerity in her deep brown eyes that set it apart.

He shot her a wink. "Anytime, kid."

Kira grinned. "Kid, huh? Well, this *kid* has a special favor to ask you."

Anything. "Oh yeah? And what's that?"

"I need a model. I'm a little rusty where studio pictures are concerned, and I need to test out my camera and light settings.

Find the best way to adjust them for different backgrounds. All that jazz."

Enlightenment pooled in as Anthony suddenly processed what she was saying. "Did your granddad leave you the studio?" he asked, stunned.

There was that beautiful smile again. "Yeah, he did. Can you believe it?"

No, he couldn't believe it. Nothing this lucky ever happened to him. Anthony shook his head. "Wow," he managed. "That's good news." He wasn't kidding either. It was the best news he'd heard in a long time. Kira Moretti was moving into town and opening shop right across the street from him.

"So is that a yes?" she prompted, snatching a sugar packet from a container nearby. "You'll let me take some test shots of you?"

Everything about the idea made him nervous. There was nothing worse than posing for the camera while the photographer zoomed in who knew how close. Still, he was no dummy. When a woman asks for help, you give her help. And spending a little time with *this* woman … well, the pleasure would be all his.

CHAPTER 4

"Thanks again for letting me take some pictures of you," Kira said as she walked a small family toward the front of the studio. Kate and Cam, both schoolteachers at the elementary, had been heading into the diner right as Kira left. With two young children in tow, they'd looked like the perfect candidates to freshen up her group sitting techniques.

"Thank *you*," Kate said, shooting her husband a look. "I've been trying to get a family picture taken for years. We'll have to come back for a full sitting soon. I'm just waiting for Cam to shave his beard," the woman mumbled.

After seeing them out, Kira strode over the hardwood floors along the window front, peering into the windows of the diner across the street. A rash of goose bumps spread over her arms as she recalled the way Anthony had winked at her. Talk about *gorgeous*. She had often wondered about the cute kid from the diner. The one she used to sneak off with.

He sure had filled out. The muscled contours of his chest

had been obvious, even through the kitchen whites he wore. As far as she could tell, he was still single—flirtatious, no ring. *Slow down, Kira.* Sheesh, she'd spent all of twenty minutes with the guy and already she wanted to date him.

This was the kind of thing that had been her downfall in life. Being distracted by the shiny new idea in her head. She could kick herself for letting Monty break her the way he had. *Stupid Monty.* She should've known better than to trust that snake. He'd taken the one thing she was good at and ruined it so thoroughly she'd almost abandoned the craft altogether. In reality, she *had* abandoned it, until now. Which was why she was so rusty.

She wondered if Anthony had taken over the diner or if he and his father ran the place together. A band of pain tightened around her heart at the thought; Gramps had wanted that very thing. He'd put her up in the duplex, even. Offered to mentor her. Teach her everything he knew so she could take over one day. Kira could've spent the last three years by his side. Years that ended up being the very last of his life, and now he was gone.

She'd missed out on that knowledge, but more importantly, she'd missed out on time with him. So why had Gramps given her a second chance? People usually didn't do things like that. Take a gift they'd given someone and—after the recipient tossed it aside—pick it up, dust it off, and place it right back into hands.

Of course, she was older now. And she hoped—as the saying went—wiser, too. She checked the time on the antique grandfather clock with wheels on it, a prop Gramps incorporated in his old-time, sepia-toned photographs. In just two hours, Anthony would walk through the studio door all confident with his man bun, muscles, and tatts. While Harper had been a wonderful listener, and quite natural in front of the lens, the family following had been more challenging. Two kids who—bless them—smiled like someone was asking to count all their teeth. Jaws locked, faces stiff. She'd had to break out the jokes to pull out those real smiles. But at least it had worked. Still, it would be a nice change, wouldn't it? Shooting a man with model good looks. One whose smile still had her heart chasing its own beat.

Kira still hadn't picked up groceries for the day, but that would have to wait. For now, she was dying to explore some of the other props and supplies Gramps had stashed away. She pried off her shoes, snatched a pair of white, fluffy socks from her bag, and tugged them over her feet. *Ah.* Boy, did that feel good. With Beethoven blasting from her portable speaker, she padded over to the storage closet and creaked open the door. It took her moment to realize the light had a pull chain, which wasn't easy to reach considering the massive mound of who knew what in the center of the space.

With a grip on the doorframe and a steep lean over the pile at her feet, Kira snatched the pull chain between her fingers and gave it a sharp, quick tug. The bulb let out a hollow-sounding pop as it flicked on. Kira tilted her head, looking over the large, charcoal-colored canvas covering the heap. She hunched down, secured a handful of fabric in each fist, and yanked it into the hallway at her back.

Specks of displaced dust whirled about, the sweet, musky scent floating up to her as she pulled in an invigorated breath.

A flash of memories poured into her mind as she took in the

items. An old-fashioned toy bus made of wood. Big enough for a toddler to sit on. She and Marissa had each done that very thing. Mom had the pictures to prove it. And there were Gramps's posing blocks. She could've used those on the small family she'd just photographed. Each block, roughly the size of a phone book, varied in thickness, perfect for propping dad a little taller when mom was too close to his height. Or for making the little guy kneeling in back come up just a little higher so his chin and neck would show.

There was so much to take in, Kira could hardly get her eyes to settle on just one thing. Gramps never had been the organized sort. Always seemed to have more of that mad scientist thing going on. Or maybe Picasso was a better comparison. Artists were said to be messy, weren't they? Gramps had a way of thriving among chaos. Kira, on the other hand, did not; her mind was already chaotic enough.

She glanced over the deep, dark shelves filling the walls at either side of the closet. They were practically bare, which was good news. She spent the next two hours wiping down shelves and organizing props into place. Since she hadn't brought any labels (she'd need to add those to her list), she tore up an old receipt from her purse, creating labels to organize the props.

She hadn't kept a close eye on the time, but when the small bell at the storefront chimed, Kira knew exactly who it was. And lucky her—she'd get to look at him from behind the lens for as long as she'd like.

The canvas cover nearly tripped her as she hurried over it with a few quick steps. "Hi," she burst out as she came around the corner. *Holy handsomeness in jeans and a tee.* "You made it."

"Yeah." He shifted his posture, shoved a hand into his

back pocket, and looked over his shoulder as if he were bored already. And what was this? A strap of leather, knotted at the back of his neck, dipped beneath the collar of his white tee in front. Before the shoot was through, Kira planned to see what sort of pendant hung from that strand of leather.

"Well, you are in luck," Kira said, folding her arms as she strode toward him. She looked him up and down with a nod. "I think I found a few props to go with this rebel-without-a-cause look you've got going on." And she wasn't kidding. He looked dangerous. To women who wanted to hold on to their hearts, anyway.

"Rebel, huh?" He let out a low chuckle. "What makes you think I don't have a cause for it?" His dark eyes held hers.

"*Do* you have a cause for it?"

He shot her a wink. "Guess you'll just have to find out."

Heat rushed up her neck, crept steadily toward her face until she felt it flare in her cheeks. It'd been a while since she'd flirted with a man she was actually attracted to. Kira had been born knowing how to flirt with the guys. Her mom and aunts always said so. And while that statement might be true, there was rarely any intent behind her playful teasing and raised brows.

"Let's see … I was hoping to start yours in the window ledge over here, if that's okay." She motioned to the elevated space along the storefront's massive window. A window that nearly took up the entire face of the studio.

"You mean I don't get to hop onto that wagon over there?" He nodded toward the setup by the backdrop.

"How about we save that for next time."

Anthony turned to look out the window. "Are people going to see me when they walk by?"

"Probably not," she lied.

"Oh, then what's the point?"

The two shared a laugh. "How about this," Kira said. "When you ask me a question, tell me what you'd like the answer to be, and we'll go as follows."

"What would be the fun in that?"

Kira pinned her lips and stifled a grin. "You're really going to make me work for this, aren't you?"

Anthony shook his head. "Nah, I won't. Promise. Where would you like me?" He shuffled over to the two-foot ledge and climbed up, ducking as the extra height brought him close to the ceiling.

"You're taller than I realized," she said.

"Yeah, I've grown a little since grade school," he said.

Yes, he had. "Go ahead and sit on the floor with your back against the brick, and your legs stretched out before you." She dashed over to where her tripod stood and unfastened the camera by twisting the small knob that secured it. Once it was free, Kira looped the sturdy strap around her neck and headed back toward the window.

She walked quickly at first, anxious to get to work, but as her gaze settled over the sight in the display window, she slowed. Her breathing did, too. When one stumbles onto a wild buck in its natural habitat, the last thing they want to do is scare it away and ruin the view. She stopped in place, lifted the camera, and looked at him through the viewfinder. With the slightest turn of the ribbed lens, he came into sharp, glorious focus.

The rustic brick wall at his back had nothing on his muscular arms and chest, the contours visible even through his tee. Head tipped back, eyes closed, chin lifted enough to reveal the outline of his well-defined jaw. He must have showered between his shift at the diner and coming here, because his black hair was damp, which—with its length and slight wave—added to his appeal all the more. And while one leg was stretched straight before him as she'd instructed, the other was bent at the knee, revealing a perfect tear in his jeans. If hallelujah choirs existed in her head, they were singing their praises in that moment. He was one of God's creations, after all.

She snapped a picture, zoomed in a bit more, and captured another one. Kira paused to look at the small digital screen. *Dang,* she'd cut off part of his leg in the full-body shot. That was a shame, seeing that he'd worn a rather good-looking pair of cowboy boots. She was rustier than she thought. Kira stepped back, widened the angle, and snapped a few more. The outdoor lighting was perfect, pouring in from the window to accent his features. *Wow.* Talk about magazine ready.

She ducked behind the lens once more and zoomed in on his face as she took a few steps closer. He was one of those guys who gave five-o'clock shadow a good name. The short, dark scruff accented the masculine cut of his jaw and chin. The pendant was showing now—a small wooden cross, rough around the edges as if it'd been hand carved.

At once, Anthony's eyes opened. He pulled his head away from the wall and set his eyes on her. "Tell me when you're ready, I guess," he said, his demeanor shifting.

"What do you mean?" she asked.

"I mean, am I supposed to look at you and smile like a cheese ball, or what?"

Kira chuckled. "That wasn't exactly the direction I planned to give you," she said, glancing at the shots she'd taken so far. The frame on those offered a lot more wiggle room for cropping. "I was sneaking a few candid pictures in while your eyes were closed. I hope you don't mind."

"You were?" He brought a hand up to his chest. "I feel violated."

"Shut up," she teased, encouraged by his playful nature.

"So is this your lucky music or are you just trying to *set the mood?*" He'd lowered his voice for that last part.

"Oh," Kira said, realizing she still had her phone going in the background. "My mind has the tendency to wander," she explained. "I mean, really—some days it's all over the place. *This* just helps keep it under control. Like reins on a wild horse."

He grinned. And it was a shame she hadn't had the camera poised, because it was brilliant. "A wild horse. I like that."

With the slow exhale of a very deep breath, Kira forced her mind back on the task before her. A wonderful one at that. She could spend hours taking pictures of a guy like Anthony. It was safe to say that—for the next little while—keeping her mind from wandering would be a breeze.

CHAPTER 5

Anthony couldn't remember being so self-conscious. It felt like he was back in junior high, passing the girls' tennis team on his way to wrestling. Overhearing giggles and whispers. Of course, all he could hear now was the occasional click of the camera when the music waned, but who knew what Kira was thinking on the other side of that lens?

She *had* done a fair amount of flirting, complimenting everything from the ink on his "buff biceps" to the "loose natural wave" of his "Banderas-like hair." Kira Moretti knew how to reel a guy in, and Anthony couldn't help but go along for the ride. Not that he wasn't leery in love after his bad experiences, but he hadn't sworn off it completely. Call it hope or youth or pure foolishness, but he was starting to wonder if Kira was the reason he'd been compelled to stick it out here in Cobble Creek. After all, Mr. Moretti had been disappointed when—after Kira finally made it out there to apprentice for him—Anthony had been off chasing Elsie. "*If you would've just stuck around, she might not have left,*" he'd said. And while his voice had carried a teasing tone, Anthony got the impression that Angelo had truly hoped the two might hit it off.

"Wow, you are off in another land, aren't you?"

Anthony shook his head, then ran a hand over his face before setting his gaze on Kira. "Another land?"

She lowered the camera and grinned. "Yeah. What's holding your thoughts?"

"Just ..." He shrugged. "Remembering the time you came out here to see about taking over for Angelo. How I was gone during that time."

Kira cradled the camera base in her palm as she lifted the strap up and off of her neck. She strode over to an open metal case. Black foam padding filled the bottom layer, save for a space the size of the camera carved out in the center. "Yeah." She nestled the body of the camera into the protected spot and draped the strap over top. "Gramps was pretty upset that you were gone."

"He was?" Anthony had lost track of how many times Angelo had talked about Kira, but he hadn't known if the man ever talked to Kira about him.

She closed the case and hoisted it into a nearby cabinet. "Oh yeah. I always got the impression he was hoping to set us up."

Anthony felt that one in his toes; turns out it wasn't just in his head. He shot her a wink. "Smart man."

"Very," she agreed.

Anthony couldn't decide which he liked best—the way Kira agreed so quickly, or the smile she wore in the process.

"Well ..." she said, padding over to the studio lights and

clicking them off. A shallow *pop* bounced off the hardwood, one after the next. "I'm starving. Want to get a bite to eat?"

"Sure," he said. "Sounds good to me. If you're up for some pizza, I know of a nice place in Duckdale Hollow next to the bowling alley. We could play a few games too, if you're up for it." He gulped, hoping the offer wouldn't scare her away.

"Bowling? Man, I haven't knocked pins since I was, like, sixteen."

Anthony shot her a look. "Knocked pins?"

"I mainly had *guy* friends in school. That's what we always called it." She ran a hand along the back of her neck, nodding. "Well, if you don't mind following me to the duplex, I can pull on a pair of jeans before we go."

"Not at all," he assured. "We can take my car from there, since Duckdale's about thirty minutes from town." He patted at his pockets before remembering the jacket he'd removed. "Want any help closing things down in here?"

Kira spun slowly in place before setting her eyes back on him. "Nope. Think we're ready to rock."

❧

Yep, she still had it. Kira had gotten a gorgeous guy to ask her out on her second night in town. And not just *any* gorgeous guy. One who might possibly be the real Italian deal. She tugged on her favorite pair of knee-torn jeans before snatching her tan cowgirl boots off the floor. At the window, she pried the metal blinds to see Anthony's shiny black truck waiting in the driveway, the sight visible thanks to a nearby streetlamp.

A quick shirt change allowed for an extra layer of

deodorant, just in case, and soon she was out the door and wondering why she hadn't bothered to grab her jacket. Already the sun had set, and night had already proven to bring a layer of frost with it.

Anthony hopped down from the truck as she stepped along the narrow walk. "You look nice," he said.

"Thanks."

He reached to open the passenger door for her, and the words *that's not necessary* worked their way up Kira's throat so quickly they'd almost snuck off her tongue. But she bit them back; Gramps would be furious if she stopped a guy from acting like a gentleman. Even if she *could* open her own door just fine.

Climbing up was a different story. The tires were nearly as tall as she was. Kira accepted Anthony's hand as she climbed onto the running board and grabbed the handle inside to steady herself. Once she was seated, Anthony closed her door and walked back to his side in the glow of the headlights. A longhaired James Dean with muscled arms and cross tattoos.

"So," she said once he was settled behind the wheel. "Couldn't find the T. rex tires?"

He glanced over while shifting the gear into reverse. "What was that?"

"I mean they must have been out of the T. rex, since you got the rare giganotosaurus wheels."

"Ah …" He tipped his head back. "But if I had smaller tires, I wouldn't get to help a lady into my truck, now, would I?"

Kira rolled her eyes, secretly loving his accent; it sounded good on him. "So were you born in Brooklyn?" she asked, recalling what Gramps told her.

"Yeah," he said. "But we didn't stay there for long. My mother wanted to own a small-town diner. Serve up good old-fashioned American food. My old man, who was running an Italian sub shop, wanted to make her dreams come true. So he put the place up for sale, gave up his own dream to help her accomplish hers." He flicked on his blinker and took a right at the end of Chapel Street. "She wanted to be as far away from Brooklyn as she could get—not sure why. She had her heart set on living in the country. Own a couple horses. I don't know, just have a different life, I guess." He shrugged.

"My old man was the pleasing type, you know? He wanted her to have it all. So he found the perfect place. Had everything she could've wanted and more. But I don't know, I guess it wasn't what she wanted after all."

Kira felt a frightened prick in her heart. It was something she'd feared about herself. Was *she* the type of person who would never be satisfied, or would she be able to settle down and be content with life here in Cobble Creek? Only time would tell. "So what happened?" she asked, her voice soft.

"About two years into it, I'd just started elementary school, I believe, she suddenly wanted something else. A whole new life … again. This time she wanted to move outside of the US and live on an island. Go off-grid, as they say, without modern technology and all that."

"Wow," Kira said. "And did she do that?"

Anthony's jaw tightened. His dark brows turned hard. "Yep. And if that didn't stick, she didn't bother letting us know. We lost track of her. I wasn't even able to get hold of her for my dad's funeral."

"I can't imagine that. I'm sorry."

"My dad used to say she must have picked Cobble Creek for us. She may not have taken to country life, but he couldn't picture a softer place to land." Anthony shrugged. "When he died, I was lucky to be surrounded by good people. In addition to your granddad, I had folks from church and the diner. Gordon Graham, the pharmacy owner. Chuck and Don, couple of old guys who sneak out for a greasy morning breakfast before they golf together Saturday mornings." He shot her a look. "I say *sneak* because their wives would have a conniption if they knew they were eating bacon and sausage behind their backs. And they refuse to entertain our low-calorie options. Sounds like they get enough of that at home."

Kira chuckled. "Guess we've all got our secrets."

"*Do* we, now?" Anthony lifted a brow.

She tried to squelch the smile that spread over her lips at his insinuative tone. "Oh, you can just stop it right there, Sparky."

"Sparky?"

"I can see right where you're going with this, but it won't work. I'm not dishing any dirt."

Anthony stretched an arm over the back of the seat, kept a light grip on the wheel. "First you tell me you've got a secret, and then you say you've got dirt to dish, and if I put those together I can only assume you've got a *dirty secret.*"

"I don't," she assured. "Just a bunch of … dumb ones, really."

"Dumb secrets are my favorite," he said, earning another laugh from her.

A deep sigh followed. Anthony's issues were different; being abandoned by a mom, losing a dad, those were hardships brought on by circumstance. Things he couldn't have avoided.

And here he was, making the best out of it. Kira, on the other hand, had made her own messes.

"I don't even think you could call them secrets," she said. "My stuff's just ... out there."

"Okay," he said. "I'm listening."

Dread washed over her like an acid bath. Why ruin her chances with the guy before he had a chance to fall for her? But then a thought came to mind. "Hey, why were you gone during that time? When I came and stayed with Angelo?"

"Ah—I guess if I have a dark secret *that* would be it. Or at least, it's a mistake I wish I hadn't made." He looked over and seemed to inspect her for a bit before setting his eyes back on the open road. "How about this? We put the heavy talk on hold, skip to something lighter while we eat, then put this back on the table at the bowling alley. Deal?"

Kira nodded, relieved that she wasn't the only one with an imperfect past. Already, it made Anthony more real than he'd appeared a moment ago. "Deal."

CHAPTER 6

Anthony leaned back in his seat before reaching for his red-tinted plastic cup. The root beer was long gone, but the ice remained. He tipped it back and let a few ice pebbles tumble into his mouth.

"I would never have guessed we'd find pizza this good in Wyoming," Kira said, reaching for her own glass. "Steaks, yes. Comfort foods, sure. But pizza?"

Anthony grinned. "I'm glad you liked it. I know what you mean. But this place really has it all. If it's not in Cobble Creek, whatever *it* might be, you're sure to find it in Duckdale Hollow. And it's nice because it's only thirty minutes away."

"That *is* nice." She shook a few ice pebbles into her mouth before scanning the room.

Duckdale's Pizzeria had an entirely different feel to it than the diner. While Tony's Diner relied heavily on bright light—either natural or florescent—this place offered a pub-type ambiance.

The place was what he'd call dark overall, with scarce lighting placed along the walls while candlelight glowed at each table, whether occupied or not.

Tonight, he liked the low light. It made things feel more intimate. Private.

Throughout dinner, the two enjoyed playful banter and light conversation, just like he'd suggested. But as they finished up, he figured it was time to tap into something more.

"So you just have the one sister, is that right?" he asked.

"Right," Kira said with a nod. "It's me; my dad; my older, more responsible sister, Marissa; and of course, half a dozen aunts and a list of great-aunts that goes on forever."

"So, lots of women, huh?"

She nodded. "Thanks to a few guy cousins, the Moretti line won't stop here. But I'm still hoping for a few little ones of my own, keep the line going on this end too—even if they don't take on my last name."

Anthony grinned, a bit of warmth stirring in his belly. He liked hearing that Kira planned to start a family some day. It was hard not to get ahead of himself, as he had the tendency to do. Especially considering it took a certain type of woman to appreciate small-town living. And it seemed they were becoming a rare sort.

"What about you?" she asked. "Do you plan to have kids? Maybe have a little bambino to take over the diner for you one day?"

He nodded. "Definitely." Though Anthony knew that desire alone didn't mean it would happen. His father may have gotten part of what he wanted, but he'd lost something very important along the way. And whether his old man accepted it or not, Mom's leaving was no fault of his own. "What do you say we go ... how did you put it—knock pins?"

Kira crunched on her ice. "Sounds good to me."

As they left the restaurant, Anthony rested a hand at Kira's lower back. And though the fabric of her blouse was cool, warmth radiated from her skin just beneath it.

Kira nudged into him, gently, as they took slow, lazy strides across the lot. A soft, tangy scent filled the breath he inhaled. He could swear it helped curb the briskness of the air. Warm, sweet, and tempting.

"Thanks again for the pizza," she said. "I wonder if they'll deliver to Cobble Creek."

Anthony snagged his keys from his pocket and gave the unlock button a press. "They do," he assured, "for the right price."

She laughed. "Then I guess I better start booking some sittings." She took his hand and climbed into the passenger seat. "Of course, I *do* know of this quaint little diner across the street from me. I've heard their food isn't too bad."

Anthony gently closed her door, then shook his head in disapproval from the other side of the glass.

Kira only grinned. Unrepentant, that one. He made his way behind the wheel and fired the thing up as she spoke up once more. "I've heard that one of the best things about the diner is the good-looking guy who owns the place."

Anthony stretched his arm across the seat, glancing over his shoulder as he backed out. "Is that right? So do you agree with them—that the owner's attractive?" He shifted gears, cranked the wheel, and weaved through the cars parked in the lot.

"He's all *right,* I guess." She laughed. "You know you're gorgeous, rebel boy."

After following the bending road toward the bowling alley, Anthony scanned the packed lot. "Maybe we should've considered that it's Saturday night. It's going to be pretty crowded. Are you sure you still want to bowl?"

Kira shrugged. "Sure. If you are. A little crowd never hurt anyone. In fact, some people *enjoy* being in crowded places."

"True," Anthony said as he pulled into an empty stall. He shut the engine off and turned to face her. Beside the truck, a towering sign stood. A giant bowling ball with a cluster of scattering pins flashed and glowed. The light grazed Kira's pretty face as he asked her one very important thing. "Are *you* someone who likes big crowds?" He gulped once the question left his lips. Already his heart was pounding out some sort of drumroll for the response.

Kira glanced up at the flashing pins before setting her eyes on him. "Of course," she said. "I'm as *extrovert* as it gets." She unlatched her buckle and pushed open her door before Anthony had time to think. Suddenly she was climbing down. She peeked into the cab of the truck, the lower half of her body out of sight due to the height of his truck. "Stay there," she said. "It's my turn to come get the door for you."

Her comment earned a reluctant chuckle, but inside, Anthony was working to digest Kira's comment. *An extrovert to the max? Loved big crowds?* She'd never last in Cobble Creek.

Suddenly his door flew open, revealing a very beautiful woman with a contagious smile extending an arm toward him. "The pins await us, my champion. Shall we?"

Another laugh snuck out. "Sure." Anthony would follow

through with the night, and he'd enjoy it as best he could. But should he bother getting to know her? Risk losing his heart to someone who'd flee Cobble Creek before the next New Year came around? He wasn't so sure that he should.

CHAPTER 7

The sights and sounds of the bowling alley breathed life into Kira. Country tunes played in the background somewhere, heard only between the loud clatter of exploding pins, beeping arcade games, and exuberant cheers. It took a little while to get their shoes and a few minutes more to get their lane, but at last it was time to play.

"I'll get our names entered into this thing while you go pick me a lucky ball." She hovered over the keyboard, squinting to read the directions on the glowing screen.

"Wait," Anthony said. "You actually trust *me* to pick out your ball?"

She took her eyes off the screen, back to his handsome face. "Sure. Get a ten-pounder, will you? My thumbs are too big for anything smaller." Kira had long ago gotten over the fact that she—unlike most of the girls she'd been on group dates with—didn't have dainty, child-like thumbs. Marissa always said it was her own fault for popping her knuckles.

At the blinking cursor, she tapped Anthony's name into the open space, but then changed her mind. A quick few taps on the delete key allowed her to give it another try. *Rebel boy.* In the space below, she tapped out something for herself: *Angel girl.*

In the spinning chair, she twisted to scan the place for Anthony. He was hunched before a display of bowling balls, inspecting the selection with caution. Yet her attention shifted to a couple of young women walking directly toward him, the two seeming to conspire as they approached in a huddle. One wore a miniskirt and baggy shirt, while the other wore jeans and a tube top. *Miniskirt* reached out and tapped his back.

It was like watching a good show. The suspense that kicked in as Anthony spun to look over his shoulder. Jealousy wasn't much of an issue, seeing that the girls couldn't be too far from their teens. Under twenty-one, for sure. The one who'd tapped him said something Kira couldn't decipher, but whatever it was made the tube top girl mad enough to give her a seething glare. Anthony looked like a kitten trapped in a pit bull's playground. He shrugged, that bashful-looking grin pulling at his lips, and then pointed over to Kira.

Two heads whipped in unison as they scanned the lane with narrowed eyes. Kira raised a hand in the air and grinned. She set her eyes back on Anthony. "Did you pick me a good one, babe?" she hollered.

Miniskirt scrutinized Kira from head to bowling-shoe-covered foot before nudging her friend's shoulder and walking away. Poor girls. Least they had good taste in guys. Anthony was probably used to being the best-looking guy in the bunch. Easy on the eyes and soft on the heart.

At least, he seemed that way. It was possible the guy was a

real heartbreaker. But something told her if that was the case, he wasn't *setting out* to hurt anyone. Her granddad wouldn't have been so fond of him otherwise. But there was something in those dark brown eyes of his. And that wide, genuine smile that lured a dimple from hiding nearly every time. That same grin he was aiming toward her in that very moment.

Her heart responded like he'd shot darts at it. A heated sort of ache. *Whoa.* He might be more trouble than he let on. Whether it was on purpose or no fault of his own, there was no doubt Anthony Marino had definitely broken his share of hearts.

He turned back to the selection, snatched a tie-dye-looking ball off the rack, and straightened up. His eyes caught hers as he walked back, but darted off to the crowd after a blink. Shyly. For someone as flirtatious as he was—and the guy *did* know how to flirt—he shied easily, too. And heaven help her, Kira was a sucker for a guy she could affect in such a way.

She stood up as he neared, then placed her palms out in waiting before her. "Is that the luckiest one in all the land?" she asked as he rested it in her hands.

"It is now," he said with a wink.

More zings to the heart. "Where's yours?"

"To make things even, I figured you'd pick it out for me."

"Brave, aren't we?" she said. "All right. I'll be right back." She gave him a nod, let her shoulder graze his as she walked by, and set her sights on the rows of balls. Would there be one that reminded her of him? A certain look to it, maybe? But then she saw it. A gray sixteen-pounder with a white skull and crossbones. A crimson rose sprouted from one of the empty eye sockets while a thorny green vine twisted its way around the entire skull. *Perfect.*

It was heavier than she'd have guessed, and the grip holes were spaced so widely apart that she had to carry it over like a baby, one arm wrapped snuggly around it with the other beneath it.

Anthony had taken a seat at the monitor, his back to her as he faced the screen. Kira shifted her gaze up to the larger, overhead screen that displayed their scorecard. The cursor flashed next to where she'd typed the names. He was back-spacing. She stopped walking, watching as he erased the *l, r, i, and g.* Once the word *girl* was gone, he typed something new. She watched, unable to hold back a grin as the word appeared one letter at a time: *woman.* She looked up to see that he'd changed his name too. No longer the rebel *boy,* but the rebel *man.*

He spun back and shot to a quick stand once he was through, looking proud of himself as he folded his arms over his chest and looked up at the large screen.

"Didn't like that I called you a *boy?*" she asked, stepping behind the rotating chair.

Anthony spun around. "I'm not a boy. And you …" he said, giving her a once-over that made her face flush. "Are *all* woman."

She gulped hard. "Well," she managed, "I can't argue with that …"

"Good." He nodded to the heavy thing cradled in her arms. "I like the ball you chose."

Kira forced her mind out of its daze. "Oh, yeah. The design on here made me think of you."

"Let me guess," he said, eyes narrowing as he took the ball and studied it for a blink. "Because I'm dangerous?"

She chuckled. "It looks kind of like one of your tattoos."

Anthony looked over his shoulder and pulled the sleeve up on his arm. "This one?" he asked.

She nodded, leaning to inspect it further. "Yes. Because of the roses, I guess." From a distance it looked more like a scenic sketch of flowers, grass, and trees. But a closer look said there was more to the picture than that. "Is this a graveyard?" she asked, realizing.

He nodded.

She lifted a hand, traced over the main headstone with the tip of her finger. "Want to tell me about this?"

Anthony glanced down at it. "I was having a hard time saying goodbye to my mom, you know? Like, accepting that she might never come back. As a kid I had a therapist tell me, and my pops too, that we should have a service for her, as if she'd died or something. And the odd truth is, she *could've* been dead, for all we knew. How could we have known, if she insisted on living outside civilization? Neither one of us could ever really do it, though, you know? Cuz we kept on hoping that maybe she'd … I don't know, she got sick of being in places after a couple years, it seemed. It made sense to assume she'd get sick of island living and come back sometime.

"Anyway," he said, nodding toward their lane before walking over to it. He set the ball she'd picked out on the stand. "Once I was eighteen, I decided it was time to stop hoping for that. I told myself that she was probably dead in the literal sense. She *had* to be to stay away so long. So if you look closely, you'll see the headstone has three M's on it. Stands for *my mother Maria.* It might seem odd to have this tattooed on my arm when I don't even know whether she's dead or alive, but … it doesn't represent putting the deceased to rest. Just my expectations of ever seeing her again."

"Wow," Kira managed. "It's so tragic that she's missed out on your whole life. If she's alive somewhere, I'm sure she's drowning in regret."

Anthony smeared a palm over his forehead. "Who knows?" He glanced over his shoulder, the action pulling Kira from her reverie. "Let's get started. Shall we?"

Kira nodded, realizing they'd gotten caught up in the same topic twice now. And she had yet to reveal much about herself. Hopefully she could avoid doing so for while longer. "Yep," she said. "Let's do this."

❧

The parking lot at Duckdale's Bowling Center had cleared out since they'd arrived. Anthony hadn't planned to stay so long. It had just happened. And now, after three games of bowling, countless pinball rounds at the arcade, and a couple of stale churros, they were back in the cab of his truck.

As Anthony roared up the engine, Kira flicked down the visor and reached into her purse. He watched as she pulled out a tube of ChapStick and spread it over her full, pouty lips. She blotted them together before shooting him a grin. "Want some?"

Why did it feel like she was asking something other than what she'd asked? "Sure."

She looked at him pointedly, plopped the ChapStick back

into her bag, and leaned across the seat until they were face-to-face. Anthony's pulse hammered, the chaos of it nearly as loud as the explosion of pins in the lane.

She grabbed a handful of his shirt like she'd done by the pond so many years ago, and pressed her lips to his. Only this was not the hurried kiss she'd planted on him before. This was a slow, sensual taste of something he was sure to want more of until the day he died.

She pulled back, tilted her head as she caught his gaze. "Is that good? Do you have enough?" She rubbed her lips together.

ChapStick. She was talking about ChapStick. Anthony shook his head, slipped a hand up the back of Kira's neck. "Not yet," he mumbled, moving in for her kiss once more. Fire roared in his belly, hotter than the engine as it revved.

Not too far, he reminded himself; Angelo Moretti would have his head if he moved in too quickly on his granddaughter. The thought was enough to pull him out of his daze and end things with one last kiss.

Kira looked at him, her brown eyes smoldering in the low light.

Anthony rubbed his lips together. "Think that'll have to do for now."

A smile stretched across her face. One that unraveled every rational line of thought he had. She sighed, scooted back to her side of the truck, and clicked her buckle. "Ready," she said.

Ready? Oh, that meant he should pull out of the lot and steer them back to Cobble Creek. A part of his brain must've caught on, because soon he was nodding and putting the truck into gear.

"I forgot to ask about those girls," Kira said as he pulled onto the street. "What did they say to you when you were picking a ball out for me?"

Anthony would have to focus very hard if he wanted to pull his mind off that warm, delicious mouth of hers. He put his thoughts back on the alley, recalling the pair who'd approached him after they'd arrived. "Oh, they were just ..." He paused, chuckled, then puffed out his chest. "They wanted a little instruction on their game. Wondered if I'd come over and personally coach them on their techniques."

Kira laughed. "You're kidding. From where I was standing, they looked like they'd barely graduated from high school."

He nodded. "Yeah, they looked young to me too. Maybe that's why I had to go fix things on the scorecard. Can't have anyone thinking I'm a mere *boy*. Or that I'd be interested in anything less than a *woman*."

"Hmm ..." She nodded, turned to look out the window. "So what did you tell them?"

"I explained that I was already *instructing* someone for the night."

She laughed. "Too bad I whooped you two out of three."

"An instructor," he said with a grin, "always lets his student have a taste of victory before the day is done."

Kira slapped his arm. "Well, I had two tastes of it."

Anthony stopped at the red light, let his gaze fall to her lips. "So did I." Was it just the streetlight, or did his insinuation make her blush? It made her smile in the least of it.

"I had a lot of fun tonight," she said. "I like knowing there's a decent-sized city not far off from Cobble Creek. It makes me think I might actually be able to live in a small town."

He nodded. "Good to know." In truth, it caused that spark of fear to flare up in him. Was he a fool to get involved with a woman who might be here today and gone tomorrow? It brought his mind back to their plan to talk more about their pasts while they bowled. It wasn't that he'd forgotten about it. And he was pretty sure she hadn't either. It was just … sometimes it was better *not* to know. If things between them were destined to fail, it wouldn't be such a crime to delay that knowledge for now and have a little fun. It'd been a long time since he'd given in to the urge to kiss a woman like that. It felt good.

"Man," Kira said with a yawn. "I'm tired. It's been a long day. *Oh,* and I forgot to pick up some coffee grounds."

"We can stop and get some at the market," he offered. "I'm not pressed for time." He glanced at the dash, noticing it was already after midnight. There wasn't a market open in Cobble Creek that late, but there were two options in Duckdale. Riverside might be an option too …

"No thanks," she said. "I'll just go after church tomorrow."

Anthony glanced over, guessing she planned to attend the church Angelo went to, which was his too. "You going to the one up there by the Country Quilt Inn?" he asked. "They have really good coffee there. I should know; I'm the one who provides it."

She glanced over. "Is it the same as what you gave me at the diner this morning?"

He nodded, hoping that'd be a good thing. "You can even bring your own mug and fill her up. Lots of people do that."

She looked satisfied. "Hmm. Maybe between the diner and the church, I won't have to brew my own coffee."

He liked that idea. "I'll give you the same deal I gave Angelo," Anthony said.

"And what's that?" she asked.

"Free coffee. Just for coming in to see me."

She scrunched her face up. "You mean I have to actually come in and *talk* to you? I can't just, like, call ahead and have a busboy rush out for curbside delivery?"

Anthony shot her a glare. "You're terrible."

"I know," she admitted with a laugh. "I hope you don't mind that we sort of skipped the whole *reveal-all-the-crap-from-our-past* talk tonight. I'd kind of like you to get to know me first. You know, who I am now, not who I *was.* Since I'm making efforts to change."

"I don't mind at all," he said. "We've got plenty of time." At least, he hoped they did. Still, Kira's words were—to Anthony—a marching army of red flags, urging him to retreat. His mother had tried to change plenty of times. The irony would be if the one thing that actually stuck was the life she'd chosen away from them. But it wasn't just her. Elsie and Ruth—they'd been seeking change too. And inevitably it separated them from him.

But Kira's change was different. Her efforts were what brought her there in the first place.

Just take things slow. That calming advice, heard in the sound of his father's deep voice, reminded Anthony that this wasn't a war. And it wasn't a race either. He was dealing with a very beautiful woman who had moved to Cobble Creek. One who may or may not be a good match for him. He'd take things one encounter at a time and try—very hard—not to lose his heart too soon.

CHAPTER 8

Kira scrolled down one row of pictures after the next on her computer, her heart aching as something horrible sank in: She'd been shooting in the wrong setting. The images were promising. Decent lighting, acceptable cropping, and if she said so herself, beautiful portrayals of the willing volunteers who'd taken time to let her photograph them.

Each photo had looked perfect on the camera's display screen, but sadly, the dimensions had been set for previewing only. Kira looked at the thumbnail-sized portrait of Harper on her screen, clicked and dragged out the corner, and cringed as the girl's lovely face began to pixilate, making the photo look more like a scrambled puzzle than a portrait. She scaled back, wondering if perhaps a wallet-sized picture could work, but it was no good; all the shots she'd taken on that day were unusable.

"I can't believe I did that." She scooted her chair away from the small kitchen table before striding toward one end of the dining area. And then back. Arms folded, lips and jaw tight, Kira resisted the one thing she knew she had to do. Call them. Call Cam and Kate and Frankie and her stepdaughter, Harper, who could probably go on Broadway, she had so much charm shining through her face. Kira needed to thank them for their time, assure them that the sitting had served its purpose, giving her a refresh course and all, but that she wasn't able to give them the digital images like she'd hoped. At least she hadn't charged for any of the sittings. Perhaps she could at least give them a gift certificate, since she had no photos to offer in exchange for their time.

She reminded herself that even Gramps suffered his share of mishaps. The worst being the time he'd shot at a family reunion. People had flown in from out of town, were together for just a small space of time. He was shooting with film then, and when he went to switch out the roll, he noticed the back of the camera had a hairline crack. Enough to expose the roll of film and ruin the pictures. But a miracle had happened, because the very first slide had escaped exposure. And luckily, it was a picture of the entire group. Kira could nearly hear him now, retelling the way it had been a perfect picture. The little ones were looking at the camera, most smiling, even. The great-grandmother, a woman in her nineties, had struggled to keep from hunching during the shoot, but even she looked poised and ready. The woman's dog, who'd been kenneled during the remainder of the shoot, had somehow run right in front of the group as he snapped the picture. And the family loved it.

The recollection made her breathe easier. She only wished she could salvage a few of the ones she'd taken. Anthony's pictures came to mind as Kira shuffled back to her laptop. She plopped into her chair and scrolled down to the final round of pictures she'd shot that day. If the images were life-sized, they could likely sell at every mall in the country, advertising anything from tattered jeans, beat-up boots, hair gel, or cologne. Heck, digitally place a motorcycle beside him and he'd sell that too.

Kira lingered over her favorite one of the bunch. Anthony wasn't exactly smiling, but there was a spark of amusement in his dark eyes. The slightest hint of a dimple in his roughly shaven cheek. And something that made Kira's limbs turn hot and melty. The word *dreamboat* came to mind, making her laugh at memories of Grandma Moretti using that word to explain Gramps.

She thought back on the last few days, recalling Anthony's kiss in the bowling alley parking lot. In the days that followed, he'd offered a cup of hot coffee each time she strode inside the diner. He'd been as sweet and flirtatious as he'd been on their date. *But*—and this was a big but—he hadn't asked her for another date. What was she supposed to make of that? She'd decided to skip the diner this morning and brew her own coffee, which paled in comparison like she knew it would. There was something else bothering her, too, something that indicated he might not be so into Kira after all: When Anthony walked her to the door after their perfect date, he'd simply given her a hug and kiss on the cheek. Like he might do with a friend or one of the girls who'd tried hitting on him that night.

Kira knew she was forward, that she shouldn't be the one initiating kisses on first dates, but the knowledge only frustrated her more. That's simply who she was. Playful and impulsive. If that scared Anthony away, he wasn't right for her. A conclusion she'd already come to dozens of times since their date.

She groaned and allowed her body to slump off the chair, where she spread out over the sun-drenched rug like a starfish. "Why am I the way I am?" she asked the ticking clock and dancing dust speckles. Couldn't she just be like *Prissy Marissy*, who wouldn't dream of initiating a kiss if her life depended on it? Who never even had urges to wink or flirt or smack a guy on the arm while joking with him?

Guilt caught up with her before she entertained those thoughts further. It wasn't fair to call her sister names. Especially when Marissa was like most women out there. Kira was the one who stood out like a sore thumb.

She pushed her mind back to the photo dilemma she faced. It was a good thing that—since the test shoots—she hadn't shot more than prop arrangements and scenic ideas. It didn't matter that she couldn't enlarge those; she could take what she needed from the small images. See what settings gave her the best lighting for the environment. At least she'd caught the problem and knew how to fix it. She needed to start making money off the studio, and quick.

The distinct vibrating of her phone rumbled the dining room table, causing Kira to sit up in a blink. She shot to her feet, shoved past her growing to-do list, and snatched up the small device. A text glowed bright on the screen.

Is this Studio Click?

. . .

Kira grinned as she replied with a simple *yes*.

I saw your sign about the studio reopening, and I'd like to come speak with you about an idea I have. When will you be in the studio?

Kira tapped out a quick reply. *I open today at eleven.*

Great. The reply came. *I'll see you then.*

Kira shot a fist into the air. "Woo-*hoo*!" She might get her first paying job.

She glanced at the wall clock, realizing it was time to leave already. The laptop was warm against her fingers as she snapped it closed and zipped it back into its bag. She set her planner on its designated corner of the counter, her to-do list glaring at her as she moved. While she'd crossed a few things off like *buy groceries and update the storefront marquee,* she had yet to introduce herself to the tenants next door or pull out their lease and see what the terms were. She also hadn't looked into the payment details of the studio lease. Of course, it was mid-month and probably wasn't due until the beginning of April. Same with rent. But she needed to make that a priority. *Tonight. When she got back.*

Still, as she gathered her coat and keys, Kira couldn't help but think the people next door were awfully quiet. Especially since it was a single mom and her kid. Of course, Kira listened to music a lot, so they'd likely gone unheard for that reason. Yet as she started up the car and retrieved the ice scraper Anthony gave her in the church parking lot, she realized the car in the tenant's driveway hadn't moved. No tire tracks had been made since it snowed.

A shot of fear tore through her as she wondered if something horrible had happened to the pair. Kira stopped scraping the frosty windshield and rested the bar across the hood of her car. In mere seconds she was pulling open the screen door and ready to knock. But a note on the door stopped her short: a page ripped from a spiral-bound notebook, the tattered fringe waving in a ripple from the breeze.

Had an emergency and were forced to move. Keep the car in lieu of rent. It's worth two months' worth. The title and keys are in the apartment.

Whoa. Kira was really going to have to step it up now. The title and keys may be inside the duplex, but the weight of that four-door sedan was right on Kira's chest. No more test shots and nature walks and hopes that people would walk right through that bell-chiming door. Kira needed to go out and get some business. She shuffled back to the car, careful not to slip on the ice patch along the drive, and snatched the scraper off the hood. Before buckling up, she lifted her to-do list off the passenger seat, rested it against the center of the freezing steering wheel, and scratched on yet another chore: *Put a for-sale sign on car. Find a new tenant for the duplex.*

By the time she stepped through the back entrance of the studio, Kira's head was swimming. *This* was usually the point where she started constructing an escape plan. She'd messed up on the first two hundred pictures she'd taken. She hadn't had *one* paying customer walk through her doors. And now she'd lost the only tenants she had. Plus she had some beat-up sedan to sell if she wanted to make the mortgage payment, which—for all she knew—could've been due yesterday. She wasn't used to being responsible for so many things.

A knock sounded from the front door, reminding Kira she'd forgotten to unlock it. With an odd dose of emotion rearing up to blow, she shoved her hand in her pocket and scurried toward the front. She vaguely made out a pair of denim jeans visible through the glass door as she struggled with her keys. At last she snagged the right one and shoved it into the lock. A quick turn followed by a longer, swinging hitch caused that faithful clank to sound. The bell chimed as she tugged the door open, her eyes finally moving up the potential customer on the other side.

"Hi there, kid." With kind brown eyes and a smile more alluring than kittens, Anthony Marino stepped into the studio. Cool air clung to his leather jacket while his spicy cologne added to the reasons she was drawn to him.

Filled with a sudden gratitude for her only friend in town, Kira flung her arms around Anthony's solid build. "Hi," she said. "I'm so happy to see you." She held him like that for a moment, letting his wonderful energy seep into her soul.

His arms wrapped around her in return, but soon he let them drop to where he cradled her elbows through her heavy coat. "I'm happy to see you too," he mumbled, his lips dangerously close to her ear.

Kira tugged back. "I'm having a bad … a lot of bad days in a row."

Anthony shrugged out of his jacket, concern gripping his face already. "What's the matter?"

You haven't asked me out again yet, for one … "Well, I was really happy with the test pictures I took on that first day, right? The ones I took of Harper, Cam and Kate's family, and you."

"Okay …" Anthony helped Kira remove her coat, then motioned for her to take a seat with him on the leather couch in the waiting area.

She started with the problem she'd discovered with the dimension settings, and continued all the way through the note she'd found on her tenant's door that morning.

"I'm sorry," Anthony said once she'd unleashed. "That would be discouraging."

She nodded. "Very. And—" Kira stopped short as she recalled the text that had come in that morning. She shot a quick glance at the grandfather clock and gasped. It was already twenty after eleven. "Someone's supposed to be here. I have to pull myself together." She shot to a stand, patted at her pockets, and then her hair while turning to find where she'd set her bag.

"Kira?" Anthony said, voice low and calm.

"Yeah?"

He cleared his throat, cupped a knee with his palm. "I'm the one who texted you."

She took that in for a minute. "You are?"

A half-grin pulled at one side of his lips. "I could have told you it was me, but …" He shrugged. "I *do* have a business proposal for you."

Kira felt herself relax at the knowledge. There was no strange man on his way to her studio. It was just Anthony. "Let's hear it," she said.

"I'd like you to take some pictures of the diner, inside and out. Get shots of my employees doing what they do around the place, you know? Then I'd like to frame some poster-sized pictures and replace the art hanging on the walls. I think it'd look nice, and it'll get folks interested in what's new at the studio."

Kira resisted the urge to reach out and hug him again. "Thank you," she breathed. "I'd love to do that."

He grinned. "Good. So how much would you like to charge me?"

"Whatever you want to pay. I'm just happy to have my first job."

His smile wavered. "That's fine to do with me, since you know I won't take advantage of you, but if someone else comes and asks for a similar service, are you prepared to tell them how much you'll charge?"

Kira shifted her gaze, stared blankly outside her window. "This is probably one of the reasons I should've stuck around and let my Papa mentor me." She sank back into the waiting room couch, feeling like someone had just popped her balloon. "I can't believe he still left me the studio."

"Do you mind if I ask what …" Anthony started to say, but then he left off there.

Kira gulped, realizing just what he was asking. Or what he'd *started* to ask. "It was a dumb boyfriend. I moved out here.

Planned to stay in the duplex with Gramps until I found a place of my own. He was going to mentor me. Show me everything he knew about photography, digital adjustments and enhancements, and running the studio. And it was perfect, because taking pictures was the one thing I never grew bored of. I floated around a lot. Tried ice-skating, volleyball, piano, and flute. And that's just the hobbies. By the time I was eighteen, I had worked six different jobs. Cashier, nursery attendant, waitress, hostess, cook …"

She paused there, waited for his expression to morph into the one her parents always pulled. Or Marissa and her great-aunts. Brows stern, lips puckered in disapproval. That errant headshake teeming with disgust. But it wasn't there. Not even a hint of it. Of course, Monty never judged her either, but that's because he was the same way. Anthony, on the other hand, seemed closer to the opposite.

"But even through all of that, photography was my favorite hobby. My passion versus my job, I guess you'd say. Anyway," she said, "I dated this guy Monty who changed his name to Python …" She caught a wry grin at the corner of Anthony's lip, but she couldn't mind since she was fighting back the same grin. It was humorous.

"He wanted to take pictures too, right? And before we broke up, I bought him a really nice camera and spent months showing him how to use it. He had connections to a famous designer named Finny Shea. Not sure if you've heard of her, but she owns *Punkline* Fashion and, of course, *Finny Shea* Magazine."

Anthony gave her a nod that said he hadn't heard of her but

he was still following along. Still, no puckered *you're such a mess* face.

She pulled in another breath. "He introduced me to Finny once. And she said she was interested in seeing some of my work. If she liked it, she'd fly us to Milan and see what we could do at her next runway show.

"Python and I ended up breaking things off soon after that, which freed me up in time to accept Gramps's offer to come out here … But then four months later, I got a call from Python asking me to come with him to Milan. We had scored the job."

Anthony lifted a brow. "So you shot a runway show in Milan? Sounds *prestigious*."

"That's just it," Kira said. "I was happy here with Gramps. And I didn't even *like* my ex-boyfriend anymore. But I left anyway."

Anthony gave her a nod. He held his expression together, but the lighthearted air was gone. Kira was scaring him, she could tell.

"I picked *proving myself* over happiness. I couldn't resist the chance to say that I'd shot on a runway in Milan. Like you said —it's impressive."

"So what went wrong?"

"I made a huge mistake." Kira's insides knotted at the recollection. "I shot the runway for two full days. Not only Finny Shea's work, but other designers as well. When it was time to turn our work in, I stupidly gave my flash drive to Monty, or Python, or whatever he's going by now."

She chuckled over his ridiculous names, but then the pain sank back into place. Threatening the confidence she'd built up like an axe hovered over a shiny red apple. As lovely as that confidence was, it was nothing compared to the haunting menace of her past. "Monty stole my images and claimed they were his. Finny was *really* impressed with them, too. Not only did she hire him on full time, letting me go in the process, but she initiated a relationship with him."

"Ouch." Anthony pulled in a breath through clenched teeth. "That had to hurt."

She nodded. "I even took them to court over it. I'd been cheated out of the photos, the money, the recognition … But I lost the case since I couldn't prove the images were mine without having a digital copy of them." The humiliation was like a layer of scum. A layer that worked its way back over her skin at the memory. "The hardest part of it is just … not being able to clear the Moretti name. Here I raise this big stink suing a world-renowned fashion designer, and I *lose.* I wish I could go back and not file the suit in the first place. Better to leave it alone than to taint the family name."

A sigh pulled at her throat. "It also would've been nice to show my family that I could accomplish something big. They know I was wronged and that I *might* have had some prize-winning pictures in the bunch. But I have nothing tangible to show for it. I wanted them to see that I actually had talent. Enough to take me somewhere besides a small-town studio that Gramps handed down to me."

There. She'd done it. But unlike the tasks she regularly scratched off her lists, this didn't offer that anticipated flood of relief or boost of accomplishment. If anything, she felt an increased dose of dread.

Anthony's face was unreadable as he sat there, seeming to take it in.

"I guess I was hoping to sort of start fresh, you know? Be in a place where people weren't aware of my past screw-ups."

He nodded. "I can understand that."

"So maybe it was a bad idea to share that with you, is what I'm saying." Her heart kicked back like she'd cornered it.

"Your family shouldn't hold that against you, Kira. And it sounds more like a life-lesson thing. But if it'll make you feel better, I can sort of even things out ..."

Kira quirked a brow. "I'm sure it won't compare with mine."

"If I hadn't been out there chasing butterflies of my own, I would have been here when you came the first time." He let that simmer in the space between them before elaborating. "Elsie Fischer. She was the butterfly I was trying to catch. Or maybe I was chasing the happiness I thought being with her would bring. She was probably a lot like my mom, in retrospect. She'd moved to Cobble Creek, determined to make a life for herself at a dude ranch."

"They have those here?" Kira asked.

"A few." He ran a thumb over the smooth leather surface of the couch. "Elsie wanted to learn about horses and eventually teach others how to ride and care for them. She and I started dating. I took her out to Griff's place and taught her what I knew about the animals. I fell fast and hard, something I have the tendency to do. Told myself she was perfect for me since—unlike my first girlfriend—she planned to stay put. But soon enough she started complaining about small-town life. When we didn't see eye to eye on it, she started prodding at a rebellious part of me."

"See?" Kira said. "I knew you had it in you."

"Yeah, it was my James Dean moment. Elsie kept telling me

that staying here and running the diner wasn't what I really wanted to do. That I was stuck here against my will. And I started to believe it. I started thinking I'd been forced into a life I never wanted."

"Where did she want to go?" Kira asked, folding her legs crisscross beneath her. "What did she want to do?"

"Run an aquarium," Anthony said with a laugh.

"That's a leap."

He nodded. "From land to sea creatures. Neither of which she knew anything about."

Kira swallowed hard. Anthony had compared the girl to his own mother—a woman who'd abandoned both him and his father. But if she were being honest, this Elsie sounded a lot like Kira, too. Which she hated.

"She'd found this place in Detroit. It was about to close down, so she put the rest of her money into buying it."

The sun must've broken through the clouds, because suddenly the natural light in the studio glowed twice as bright, bringing with it a warm, gold glow that enhanced Anthony's olive complexion. One that created shadows along the muscular contours of his arms.

"Since she'd poured all that money into the aquarium, I stuck around to help her get it off the ground. We replaced bulbs and fixtures, filters and glass. And refinished the floors. The whole process showed me that Elsie was right. This really was the right path for *her*. Which made me wonder if that's what was happening on some island for my mom. Perhaps it'd just taken a few tries. But something else became clear during that time: Sadly, it wasn't where *I* belonged. I missed being home. And soon that homesickness outweighed my feelings for her.

"When I look back on it, I think God put it in my heart to help give her the new start she was looking for. In return, he showed me that I didn't need to go looking for anything outside of what I already had." He glanced out the window toward the diner. "I'm glad I came back in time to share those last years with my old man before he passed. I was the only family he really had." A wistful look brewed in his eyes. "Means the world to me."

"Yeah," Kira said, the word nearly choked with emotion. "I'm glad too." Inwardly, she was thinking of how Anthony didn't have any family left. She was glad he'd found friends in the people he'd referred to, some regulars who come into the diner, and others around town. But still, it made her wonder if she'd taken her own family for granted.

"So now you've got the scoop on me," Anthony said. "At least one of them. If you ask me, it sounds like we've both made our mistakes. But you've got this nice studio to run. I've got the diner across the street. It's possible each of us has landed exactly where we're meant to be."

Kira couldn't help but envy the confidence he spoke with. Voices from her past—Gramps used to call them gremlins—told her she'd never settle down. Never enjoy a content life. And never achieve anything great in the eyes of her family.

"You didn't come over for coffee this morning." Anthony said. He looked at her through dark lashes, chin lowered, eyes questioning.

Kira scrambled for an excuse, but decided to spit out the truth instead. "I didn't want you to get sick of me."

Anthony shook his head, sighed, and leaned his elbows onto his knees. "Would you have dinner with me tonight?"

The patient sound of his voice, the way he'd presented the question rather than argue with her about what she'd said, all of it took Kira by surprise. A spritz of tingles washed over her skin and somewhere inside her tummy, too. "Yes," she said. "I'd love to."

He stood, stepped over to where he'd draped his leather jacket, and shrugged into it. "Good. We can talk about the diner shoot then," he said. "My place. I'll text you the address. Does six o'clock work for you?"

Kira nodded, still trying to catch up. He must already have her number, because he'd texted her that morning. *The sign,* she reminded herself. That's where he'd found it.

Anthony took three long strides back to the couch where Kira still sat, legs tucked beneath her. She looked up as he neared, gulped as he lowered himself, and let her lashes close as he brushed a kiss over her forehead. "See you tonight."

And as he strode out of the studio, the chime echoing over the space, Kira rubbed the goose bumps that rose on her arms, loving the effect he had on her.

CHAPTER 9

Everyone had lessons to learn in life. That's what Anthony took from his conversation with Kira. Perhaps what they'd learned so far would help them develop a healthy relationship. There was no telling if things between them would progress as he hoped, but even if they didn't, Anthony wanted to help Kira succeed. Everyone deserves to feel good about what they offer the world, even if it was simply great food and a comfortable place to enjoy it. There was value in that. And there would be value in what Kira did too. Who knew? Perhaps maintaining the quality Angelo offered at Studio Click would be enough to—in Kira's mind—restore the family name.

The funny thing was, Anthony found himself wanting to hurry things along. Get to the part where they were steadily dating and thinking of marriage and … and being in a place where he felt certain Kira wasn't going to leave.

He shook his head. What was it that had him so anxious to give away his heart? He recalled something Angelo said in response to that very question, the words coming back to him as if spoken from the angel himself: *"You've got a whole lot of love to give, son, that's all. Just watch that you don't put it in the wrong place."*

Anthony grabbed a couple of forks and worked at shredding the roast he'd prepared in the slow cooker. He nodded in satisfaction as the tender, aromatic meat separated easily beneath the tines. A glance at the clock said Kira would be there any minute, which was perfect; the au jus was ready, the fresh buns were sliced, and the sweet potato wedges were roasted to perfection.

He leaned a hip against the counter, his mind drifting back to their conversation that morning. Anthony hadn't liked seeing Kira so upset, worried over the mishap with the pictures she'd taken. But like she said, it could've been worse. At least they'd just been test shots.

A sharp chime from the doorbell pierced through his thoughts. Anthony's chest filled with a mixture of anticipation and terror. He rinsed his hands off, reached for a dish towel, and dried them on his way through the front room.

The doorknob was warm to the touch as he pulled it open, but the screen door handle felt like an ice rod. He pushed it open quickly, urging Kira into the warmth and closing the door behind her. "Whew," he said, rubbing a hand over her back. "It's colder than I thought out there."

Kira stood mere inches from him, her strawberry scent assuring him—in case seeing her wasn't enough—that she was actually there, in his home. She lifted a glass bowl of something white and fluffy and grinned. "Candy bar salad," she said. "It's got fresh fruit in it, which means it's a side, not dessert."

Dang, he liked this girl. "It is now, is it?" He inspected the plastic-wrap-covered creation as he took the bowl from her and walked it to the table. When he spun back around, Kira was already removing her coat.

Anthony stepped over in time to take it from her and hang it beside the wooden bench in the entryway.

"It's nice in here," she said, taking in the place as she slowly walked. "Oh …" She stopped in her tracks. "Forgot to take these off."

"You don't have to do that," he said.

But she scurried back toward the bench just the same. "I don't mind." She plopped onto the bench and pried off the tall cowgirl boots she wore before adjusting a fluffy pair of pale pink socks on her feet. They matched the oversized sweatshirt that hung slightly off one delicate shoulder.

She toured the place a bit more, inspecting pictures on the mantel. There were only two. "So I can tell that this is you and your dad out front of the diner," she said. "But who's in this other one? The black-and-white?"

Anthony walked up behind her. "That's my old man and his dad out front the Italian sub shop. They ran the place together before my dad moved."

Kira nodded, bringing her face closer to the pictures as her eyes narrowed. "The men in your family are handsome." She flashed him a grin. "You've got good genes."

Heat stirred low in his belly. "Thanks."

Kira folded her arms over her chest and stepped toward the bookshelf. "Remind me ... how did your dad die? Was it an accident?"

"Lung cancer, actually."

Kira's face was buried in the bookshelf. "Oh, I'm so sorry." She spun around to look at him. "That must have been awful."

"Yeah." Anthony cleared his throat, then shifted his eyes to the dinner table before the emotion kicked in. "Well, I hope you came hungry."

She looked at him for a moment, seeming to acknowledge the topic diversion. "I am," she said. "Starving, actually. And it smells amazing in here." Kira stepped closer to him, bumped him in the arm with her shoulder. "I've never dated a guy who can cook."

Anthony puffed up his chest and stretched an arm behind her back. "Well, get ready for the good life, baby, because I'm the best in town."

She giggled. "Lucky me."

After washing up at the sink, Kira helped take care of a few last-minute details like pan-frying the cut halves of ciabatta bread and dressing the salad. Soon they were seated in the dining area, food dished out, and conversation in full force: things like childhood memories, awkward first dates, and how they managed to get through those cruel adolescent years.

As they finished up, Kira plopping a second scoop of candy bar salad onto her plate, Anthony settled the details for the diner photo shoot. "Between two to four o'clock is our least busy time of day. Will that work for you?"

Kira nodded. "Sure. And I'm mainly shooting the members of your team? Waiters, busboys, owner ..." She gave him a wink.

"That's what I imagined. You think that will be good?"

She looked hesitant for a blink, but then nodded. "Yes. I think it will be great, in fact. Oh!" she blurted, wiping a spot of cream off her upper lip. "I've got some exciting news for you. I almost forgot."

Anthony lifted a brow. "All right. Let's hear it." Already, she looked so pleased with herself he had to smile.

"I talked to the secretary at Cobble Creek High School and found out that their next dance is in less than a month. It's a girl's choice dance with a fifties theme."

"Okay," he encouraged.

"Monica—that's the secretary's name—told me they didn't have a photographer yet, and if I wanted the job, it was all mine."

"That's *great* news."

"Yeah, and they have several dances throughout the school year, so I'll be able to come up with new backdrops and ideas for each one."

He smiled, absorbing Kira's warm, brilliant energy. Allowing it to soak into his soul like a soothing remedy. In the last week, Anthony had talked with Kira over coffee at the diner a handful of times, been to her studio twice, and taken her out on a date. And each time, she managed to soften his mood with her playful nature, offering fun and interest to each interaction. He guessed life didn't often get boring when Kira Moretti was around.

She leaned her elbows onto the table as she continued, her eyes wide with excitement. "I was thinking about what kids like now and how they—especially for the girl's choice dances—probably want something less formal. And with it being a fifties theme and all …" She dragged out the last word, cuing Anthony to pick up where she'd left off. He was already catching the drift.

"We could do it in the *diner*."

"*Yes*," she cheered, jumping to her feet. "If you're okay with it."

"That's a great idea."

Her smile grew wider. "I hoped you'd think so. It's not that I couldn't do them in the studio or the school, but it'd be perfect to shoot them in that far booth by the back entrance. Don't you think?"

"Yeah, I do." He loved the fact that Kira was thinking differently—talking about her plans as more of a *we* thing than a *me* thing.

"And hopefully they'll want to get some fries and shakes while they're there. Oh, and they said I could bring out handouts for senior pictures too, since graduation's coming up in a few months." Kira leaned to one side of the chair, shoved a hand into her back pocket, and pulled out a folded page. "This is a list of their dances for next year, along with their themes. The student body already sat down and arranged them."

Kira slid the paper around her plate, past the center dish where the extra meat and buns rested, and alongside the side bowl with Kira's candy bar salad. "If the one next month goes well, we could incorporate other businesses along Main Street according to the theme." She was talking faster now, her excitement building as she rested a finger on the page. "They have a Halloween dance at the beginning of the upcoming school year. Think of how cool it would be to shoot that in

Books and Nooks, that cute little bookstore on Main. Stretch webs across one of the aisles; maybe have a live tarantula climbing up a stack of books up front. Some dry ice wafting smoke just behind the couple."

"*Wow,*" Anthony said. "You've really got a good mind for this, don't you? Makes me want to go back to high school so I can get something other than those lame dance pictures where we sit there posed in front of some foam pillar and fake, dusty plants."

"Me too," Kira admitted. "But maybe we'll luck out and have a student from the yearbook staff shoot one of us together. We'll dress up as students."

"Sounds good to me." Anthony meant that. The fact that she was thinking so far ahead told him she really did plan to stick around. Make a life for herself there. Contribute to the town in a fun and unique way. He hoped she had a talent for taking photos, like her granddad. Creativity was always appreciated, but it couldn't replace the quality Cobble Creek had come to expect from Studio Click.

Stop worrying about it, he scolded himself. Angelo always said that Kira got her eye for photography from him. And leaving his studio to her proved that it wasn't just talk; the last thing he'd want to do is set Kira up to fail.

"Man," Kira said. "I totally overate. It was too good to stop. You've got to show me how to cook a roast like that."

He grinned. "Or I can just have you over for dinner again the next time you're craving it."

"That works too." She held his gaze, allowing that magic of hers to seep into him once more.

Already, he was dreading the goodbye. Wondering if she'd come into the diner for coffee the next morning. Fifteen minutes of Kira each day could cure the lonely in his life like a drug. But he wanted more than fifteen minutes.

"Favorite things," Kira blurted. "Let's list some. You start."

Anthony looked at her for a moment while his brain played catch-up. "Favorite things?"

She grinned. "Yes. Candy bar salad. There—I started us off. Your turn."

"Mango cheesecake," he blurted.

"Fluffy socks."

"Cowboy boots."

Kira tipped her head back. "Good one. They look good on you too. Um ..." She looked around the room as if it might help, but then darted her gaze back to him, her expression turning serious. "Cold. Pillows." She put emphasis on each word.

"Ah, I like that too," he said.

"You do?" Her eyes went wide.

Anthony grinned, a small laugh creeping up his throat. "It's the best."

"Well, then, today's your lucky day. Is your freezer clean?"

"What?"

"Your freezer," Kira said, coming to a stand. "Is it clean?"

Anthony stood as well and joined her as she walked toward his industrial-style freezer/fridge. "As someone who owns a food establishment, the answer to that is always yes. Force of habit."

"Perfect." She hunched down and pulled it open. "Wow. It *is* clean. Spotless." She spun in place. "Go get your pillow."

He chuckled under his breath. "It's going in the freezer, huh?"

Kira lifted her brows and grinned.

"All right, then." Anthony tipped his head, motioning that she should come with him. "This way."

Kira looped an arm through his as they strode down the hallway. "This house is bigger than it looks from the outside. It's really nice."

"Thanks." He flicked on the light as they stepped into his rather plain bedroom. Anthony's version of making the bed was more of a yank-the-top-blanket-over-the-pillows deal. Luckily he'd just done laundry; there'd be no stray tee shirt or sports shorts toppling off the corner hamper and onto the floor. He snatched the pillow and handed it over. "Here you go."

Kira brought it against her chest, hugging it as they strode back into the kitchen. "Smells like you. Do you have parchment paper?"

"Of course." He retrieved it for her, then watched as she placed a large sheet under the pillow and slid it onto a spacious rack.

"Best. Sleep. Ever," she promised.

He nodded, quietly entertained by it all. But the truth was, he wasn't ready for sleep just yet. He hoped she wasn't either. "Want to see how the Redrocks are playing?" he asked, glancing at the mounted TV.

One corner of her lip quirked.

Anthony cleared his throat. "Or we could watch a chick flick. I have enough channels in this place; I'm sure you could have your pick."

"No," Kira said. "I like baseball." She strode past him and into the front room, where the big screen hung. "The chick flick can wait for next time."

Next time. Anthony repeated those wonderful words in his head as he joined her on the couch. Hopefully they'd have a whole lot of next times to look forward to.

CHAPTER 10

Holding hands wasn't something Kira had thought much about before. But as Anthony walked her out to her car, not a cricket to be heard in the brisk night, she couldn't pull her focus off the way his large, masculine hand cradled hers. He'd come out moments ago to start her car so it'd be "nice and toasty" when she got in. So sweet.

Anthony was tall and muscled and gorgeous to an unnerving degree, but that alone wouldn't cause the fluttering swirl of her tummy as they neared her car. It had as much to do with the other things he offered. His non-physical traits. Patience, support, kindness. Along with a swagger any real rebel would envy. A cool guy who didn't have to try—that was Anthony Marino.

A lamppost down the street hummed as he leaned his back against the car, the fringe of that light barely reaching them. Anthony secured her other hand in his as Kira faced him.

"Thanks again for dinner tonight," she said. "Next time I'll cook. Or buy, depending on how brave I feel."

He smiled, his gaze dropping to their joined hands. She'd been the one to move in to kiss him after they'd gone bowling. And while Kira had enjoyed taking him by surprise as she had in planting that kiss on him, she liked even more the way he'd responded to it. Leaning in and taking charge. Would he do that again tonight, or simply offer a small peck on her cheek as he'd done after walking her to the door? The tummy twirls picked up in anticipation, moved up in ripples as her breath hitched.

Anthony wrapped his strong arms around her and pulled her in, warm against his chest. Out here in the cold, she could smell hints of fresh laundry on him, along with the tempting scent of aftershave or cologne, she wasn't sure which. She only knew it smelled spicy and masculine and wonderful.

The tip of his nose nuzzled into her neck, just below her ear. Cool and smooth and alluring. His heated breath came next, moved along her chin up to her lips, where he toyed with her, his mouth grazing over the small peaks of her top lip in a slow tease.

Kira had never been the patient type, but the anticipation coursing through her was a thrill all its own. She resisted the urge to lean in or take more, allowed the sensation to linger and swell.

At last he moved a strong hand up the back of her neck and pressed his mouth to hers in a long, glorious kiss. He tilted his head, deepening the kiss as a whimper sounded from her throat.

Whoa. Chemistry—check. There was nothing lacking in that

department. Kira sighed, Anthony's mouth weaving some sort of magic over her in a series of lingering, passionate kisses.

At last he pulled back slightly, hesitantly. "Good night," he rasped.

Kira stayed in place, relishing in the heat of his mouth just centimeters from hers.

He pressed another soft kiss to her lips. "Are you coming into the diner for coffee in the morning?"

She forced her eyes open, tipped her head back, and scrutinized him in the low light. Those dark, dreamy eyes could unravel her if she let them. "Should I?"

"If you *want* to, yes."

"Then yes. Yours is better than mine. Plus I get to watch you in action. It's hot." She chuckled since it was a funny thing to say, but it was a true statement; Anthony ran that diner like an Italian boss. Charm, grit, and good looks all rolled into one.

He opened the car door for her, and a wave of heat pulled her in. "Enjoy your cold pillow tonight," she said.

He grinned wide enough for his dimple to show. "You too, Kira."

He stood on the sidewalk, arms crossed over his muscular chest as she drove away. The sight of him in the rearview did tingly things to her insides. Perhaps this was the beginning of something real and lasting.

A stubborn voice from her past prodded and nudged at her mind, working to be heard once again. *You're not the type of person who can stay put. It's only a matter of time before you mess this one up.*

Kira gripped her left hand tighter around the leather steering wheel and reached for the radio with the other. With one quick tap, the loud bass of a familiar song pounded through the speakers. She might like classical music to help her concentrate at work, but in the car, Kira enjoyed alternative rock. Luckily, it was just loud enough to quiet the beast once more.

CHAPTER 11

Anthony eyed the array of clocks on the diner wall—a half dozen pieces featuring things like an old-time Pepsi logo, a glass bottle of Coke, and a specially made clock that read *Tony's Diner.* In just a few minutes, Kira would arrive.

"Hey, Anthony," came Trent from his spot at the bar. "Is your lady coming in today?"

"Yeah, is she?" Benny asked, lips puckered as he blew on his coffee. "And if so, why don't you fill us in on what's happening between you two before she gets here."

"Hey, hey, now, I'm not supposed to be doing any kissing and telling. You guys know that."

"Yeah, but we're not gonna tell no one," Benny said.

"Speak for yourself. Jessie and Darcy have been asking all about it," Trent admitted in a hush. "I told Jessie I'd get the details."

Anthony dunked a fresh dishcloth into a mound of hot suds

and squeezed it out. "Oh, so *that's* why you guys stuck around for a third cup of coffee."

"Actually," Trent said, "Abby kept me up half the night. I told Jessie I'd trade shifts with her, but man … I had no idea it'd be so tiring."

"That's babies for you," Benny said with a laugh. "You'll get used to it." He leaned over the counter next, hushing his voice. "Jessie and Darcy were here Thursday afternoon having their book club, and Darcy said she spied you and Kira kissing by the kitchen when she was heading to the ladies' room. Explains why you've been missing boys' night …"

The kitchen? But then it came to him—he *had* kissed her there right after she'd finished the shoot. It was short and sweet, just a stolen kiss he hoped no one had seen. Anthony wiped the smooth surface down with the hot cloth, moving it closer to where the old men sat. He leaned in, glancing around the diner before speaking up. "I don't really know what's happening between us yet. I like her, she likes me back, from what I can tell, but we haven't made anything official yet."

The men wore smiles that might look more fitting on boys in middle school. Wide, satisfied, and mischievous.

Benny nudged Trent. "Told you something was happening."

Trent rolled his eyes. "She gets coffee here every morning, Ben, of *course* something's happening."

"How would *you* know?"

"A good sheriff knows what's happening in his precinct," Trent bragged.

Anthony couldn't help but smile. He only hoped his close friends would remain in Cobble Creek with him. One day they'd all be like Chuck and Don, having a little guy time while the ladies did their thing. Anthony could see it now, the entire group —Steger brothers and all—sitting at the corner booth. Seth and Jon would gripe about how—after their sons took over Steger Construction—they changed up the logo on the marquee after all these years. Anthony would nod and grumble about how his sons wanted to change the colors of the booths, like he'd done a few years back, upsetting his own father in the process.

"*Psssst!*" someone hissed from behind.

Anthony glanced over his shoulder to see Kira peeking her head through the swinging doors to the kitchen. He lifted a finger, glad she'd come in through the back. No need to be featured in Cobble Creek's gossip sessions just yet. Trent and Benny were caught up in a round of laughter as Anthony snuck off.

Once in the kitchen, the hiss sounded again, this time from the short hallway leading to his office. He glanced down in time to see Kira disappear through the open doorway. Anthony followed her inside, only to be greeted with a display he hadn't expected. An array of easels stood along the back office wall. The tall ones rested directly on the floor, while shorter easels balanced on two high stools and a side table.

"Hello, Mr. Marino," Kira said, reaching out to shake his hand. She wore the same business-looking suit he'd seen her in when she came to the diner in search of volunteers. "I took the liberty of enlarging select images from our shoot here in the diner. Please keep in mind these are merely a dozen of my favorites, but you'll have the opportunity to scan over the entire selection if you'd like."

Anthony straightened his shoulders, playing along with the business pretense. "Very well, then," he said with a stiff nod.

Kira tilted her head, an amused grin lifting the apples of her cheeks. She stepped over to a massive, flat case that leaned against his desk on the floor; it was too big to fit anywhere else. She pulled a stack of poster-sized boards from the bag, moved to the far easel, and displayed the first image: a close-up of Jeff as he leaned over the bar with a grin. *That smile.* Kira had captured it perfectly. The almost-twenty-year-old kid had really proven himself over the years, showing that he could not only welcome the customers with a witty word, but run the diner in Anthony's absence without a hitch.

"That's a great picture," he said, reverence coating his tone.

Kira set the next two in place and stepped aside. His cooks, Howie and Lance. She'd come in early for theirs, before the diner opened. She'd captured a picture of Howie—who was in charge of the fresh rolls—kneading the dough. In the next, Lance was busy at the cutting board, the angle catching a mountain of sliced carrots and celery for their soup of the day —chicken noodle.

"You really did a great job with these guys," he said. "I like everything you got around them too. The wood grain of the cutting board, even. A bit of flour on Howie's chin. It's perfect."

Similar words came to him as she displayed the next three enlargements. Only they weren't employees; they were patrons.

"I know you wanted me to focus mainly on the employees, but while I was here, a few things caught my eye." She pointed to the first photo, a close-up of a wide-eyed baby, mouth poised behind a spoonful of chocolate shake and whipped cream. "Maddie and Bear were here with their little one. They signed a release form saying that I could use these pictures to display here at the diner, in case you decided to use them. The others did the same."

Anthony glanced at the other candid photos as she continued, "I thought that a fair portrayal of Tony's Diner should include a few patrons, since that's what it's all about. People who've been coming for years, ordering their favorite shake, snack, or burger."

Anthony took in the next picture, which featured the town's book club. The large group of ladies had been meeting at Tony's for years. In the photo, several of the women had their heads tipped back in what could only be called roaring laughter. Next was the small family that had stopped in on their way through town. They'd ordered a family-style meal; nearly one of everything lay scattered over the table.

"If you're not in love with the patron pictures, that's fine—" she started to say, but he couldn't let her finish.

"I love them."

"What?"

Anthony nodded, walked wordlessly toward the display, shaking his head in wonder. "You really do have your granddad's gift, Kira." He felt proud of her in that moment. He was beginning to really care for her. Wanted her to succeed. Not just selfishly, so she'd stay in Cobble Creek, though that was part of it. More than that, Anthony wanted the spectacular woman to know just how talented she was.

He heard a sniff before Kira cleared her throat. "You really think so?"

Anthony was surprised to see tears welling in Kira's brown eyes. "Of course," he said, extending his arms to either side.

"Come here." He wrapped his arms around her as she stepped into him.

"I guess it just feels good to hear," she said. "From someone other than my family, I mean. Whenever they compliment me, I feel like they're just trying to get me to settle on *something,* so they just encourage whatever *thing* it is I'm pursuing at the time."

Anthony tipped his head to the side. "Have you talked to them since moving here?"

She nodded. "A few times."

"But they *do* encourage you?" He'd been under the impression, by the way she'd spoken about her family, that they weren't encouraging at all.

Kira stepped back and ran a hand over her face. "It's not that they don't have nice things to say. They do. But I can tell—no matter how it comes out—that they expect me to drop out, give up, or outright fail."

Anthony had the strong urge to challenge her perception, but how could he? He simply didn't know enough yet. But there was one thing he *did* know. "It's possible they're not thinking that at all," he said. "But either way, you don't have to prove anything to them or anyone else. If you stay here and run the studio, you should do it because you're happy here. Don't you think?"

Kira nodded. "Yes."

"Good," he said. "Now let's see the rest of these pictures. I love what you've done so far."

CHAPTER 12

Kira stared up at the dark ceiling, a wide grin on her face, a cool pillow beneath her neck and head. In her mind, she drifted back to Anthony's office, watching as he admired her work, complimented her talent, and mentioned how good she was at presentation—something that gave her short stint in advertising validity after all. The supposed *detours* in her life were finally starting to come together, each assisting her in different aspects of running the studio in Cobble Creek. As business picked up, she'd likely need to bring on some help with the digital side of things, since she spent more time working on the photos then taking them. Maybe one day she'd bring on a photography assistant, but for now, Kira was happy doing it on her own.

She closed her eyes as a deep feeling of satisfaction washed over her. Kira wasn't meant to be some world-renowned photographer who traveled the world with Finny Shea. She simply needed to be herself.

And if she could do that *and* have Anthony Marino by her side, she'd be one lucky girl—woman. Anthony was proving to be everything she could want in a man. More so, considering she never realized a man could make her feel the way he did. Complete. Accomplished. Good enough just the way she was.

Of course, life wouldn't be life if there weren't a few gremlins clinging to her subconscious. If Kira had to identify the one that threatened her now, it would be concern over the duplex and the sedan her old tenant left behind. Sure, they'd told her the duplex was paid up through April, but she needed to divide her focus each day. Photography was her passion. What a beautiful, happy, and wonderful thing that was to say with such surety. She loved coming up with new ways to earn money, bring in business, and serve the charming town of Cobble Creek.

Less appealing, and by that Kira meant *way* less appealing, were things like land-lording and car-selling (she hadn't even signed up for that one), and making sure everything was paid up on time. And something she was *really* dreading, the reason she hadn't done more than post a small "for rent" sign in the front yard, was going through the other dwelling. She had to make sure the tenant hadn't left anything else behind. And she couldn't just wait for someone to call and want to see the place. That *wasn't* the time to dash over and play twenty-one pickup, as her mom used to call it. (*Hey, who can pick up twenty-one pieces of trash the fastest?)*

And while Kira knew all of these things, doing something about them was an entirely different story. It was the reason she often set herself up to fail. Well, not this time. First thing tomorrow, she would get started on that duplex. She had until eleven o'clock to open the studio. She'd be taking baby pictures for the sheriff and his adorable wife, Jessie. Her first hired job (besides Anthony) in Cobble Creek. And just like that, she had her mojo back.

She'd made mistakes in the past—who hadn't?

She wasn't perfect—who was?

But one thing she had was determination. And with that acknowledgment in full force, Kira drifted off to sleep.

CHAPTER 13

Anthony eyed the wall of clocks in the diner, guessing he had another hour before Kira showed up for her morning coffee. Heat stirred low in his belly at the mere thought of her. He was falling fast, but it was hard not to; Kira was fascinating. And she'd really blown him away yesterday. Shown him exactly why Angelo had willed Studio Click to her.

Anthony hated to admit it, even to himself, but it had been a relief. The woman really did have a natural gift. And beyond that, she had a great business sense. He hadn't expected her to put on a presentation of the images she'd shot. Heck, she even had framing bids from three different companies, each complete with special non-glare glass so the bright lights wouldn't obstruct the view of each portrait. Talk about going the extra mile.

He glanced over the old photos along the diner walls. He liked the posters of vintage cars, drive-in theaters, and the old-fashioned couple sharing a milkshake, but it was time for a facelift. Anthony could hardly wait for the frames to come in so he could get Kira's photographs in place.

The door chime rang, drawing Anthony's eyes to the front of the store. He expected to see Chuck and Don shuffling in, arguing over whose joints and back pain were worse. Instead, a brown-eyed angel stepped inside. Slender, yet curvy in her fitted jeans and a sweater, hair pulled into a bun that put his to shame. He watched as she scanned the place before her eyes fixed on him. She smiled, but something was off.

"What's wrong?" he asked as she rushed over.

Kira clutched a barstool and dragged it back a few inches. She climbed onto the stool, plopped an elbow on the counter, and sank her face into her hand, eyes closed. A strand of wayward hair bouncing as the vents kicked on overhead. "I knew I would mess this up."

The wall of clocks ticked behind her. A noise Anthony almost never heard during business hours. Yet it seemed her statement had caused everything else to stop in its tracks. The Tanners' baby went from pouting to mute. Connie and the staff from CC's Salon had been chuckling seconds ago, laughter loud enough to fill the room. But all of it stopped as Anthony took in Kira's comment. The kind of thing he'd expect to hear from someone who could walk away with their hands in the air, declaring that things never went their way. They gave it a go, the old college try, failed, and now they were packing up and hitting the road.

Kira pulled her hand from her face. Her eyes flicked open. Wide at first, but then they narrowed. "Is everything okay?" she asked. The concern he saw in her expression said he'd left his poker face at home.

He shook his head. "No. I mean, *I'm* the one who should be asking that question." Anthony had always been able to detect a lie with ease. There were things that changed in the person's face after they'd spoken it. An odd tightness in the brow. The shift in their posture. Even the feigned sincerity on their face moments before as they plotted the structure of their words. He figured that's why he was such a terrible liar himself. He could sense every tendency to do those very things as something less than true worked its way toward his lips.

He gulped as Kira searched his face, hoping she couldn't see hints of the upset happening within him. If what he and Kira had was the meager starts of a promising fortress, it was already crumbling in his mind.

"What ..." He shook his head, gulped, and dropped his gaze to a row of spotless glasses beneath the bar's ledge. "You said you messed things up. How?" His heartbeat moved to his face in hot, frantic thumps as he waited.

"I got a call from my mom this morning, who said Gramps's lawyer called her and asked for my email address. He'd sent me a few things and, when he didn't get a response, feared maybe he had the wrong one."

Anthony glanced up at her. "Okay," he encouraged.

She tilted her head. "Mind if I get a cup of coffee?"

He straightened up, working to pull out of the premature meltdown. "Of course." Anthony snatched a clean mug and filled it with the dark, aromatic brew. Perhaps he should've stuck with decaf that morning; his heart was still racing hard. He set the steaming mug down before her and slid the cream and sugar packets her way, already knowing exactly what she'd use: two packets of raw sugar and one small cup of plain cream.

Kira tore open the first packet of sugar and poured.

"So did he have the wrong email address? His lawyer?"

The next packet of sugar went in before she peeled back the foil lid of the cream. "No, I just … had no idea he'd be trying to communicate with me by email. I hate email. It's just not something I'm used to having on my radar, you know?"

Anthony shook his head in irritation. "Would you just tell me what's going on?"

Kira looked up from her coffee, eyes wide.

A tap came to his shoulder. "Just checked the inventory," Howie said. "The only thing that didn't come in with this morning's order were pickle chips. I already called and let them know."

Anthony glanced back. "Thanks, Howie."

Kira caught his gaze. She didn't have to ask; her eyes said it all. *What in the world is wrong with you this morning?*

"Sorry," Anthony mumbled. "I just … if something's wrong, I want to help you. And if I'm going to help you, I might need to shift some things around with my crew for the day."

True, but that wasn't the reason he was acting crazy. He was acting crazy because he was terrified that—as promising as things between them were—it was all about to end. It felt like she was taking her first steps toward that ominous white flag. The one every woman in his life seemed destined to wave.

"Well, it turns out that the duplex wasn't paid off *through* April; it was only paid off *to* April, meaning the payment was due a few days ago. There's a grace period, so I don't technically have a late penalty yet, but the concern was that I hadn't even registered an online account, which is how I'm supposed to pay, so …" She shrugged, seeming to relax slightly, and brought the mug to her lips.

"We need to get your place rented out."

She nodded behind the mug.

"And that car sold."

Another nod.

This was something Anthony could work with. His shoulders lifted. "What have you done to advertise the rental?"

"Just stuck a yard sign in the grass. But I was thinking that I could post a few flyers on the telephone poles along the street."

Anthony shook his head, containing a chuckle in his throat. "Don't do that. We had a big issue come up with Trent when he came into town—the sheriff. We can't staple anything to those poles."

"Oh, that reminds me! I'm supposed to shoot baby pictures of the sheriff's daughter today at eleven. I *can't* forget that."

"No, you won't." He wouldn't let her. "Is the rental ready for someone to move in?"

Kira shrugged. "I haven't been inside yet."

Anthony felt his eyes widen.

"Don't judge me," she said with a laugh. "I've had a million things going on. And in my defense, I thought I had until May to worry about payments. I've been focusing on the studio."

Anthony wiped the judgment off his face in a flash and glanced at the clocks once more. "Here's what we're going to do. We have a little less than five hours before your sitting. I'll let Howie take over for me. I'll grab a few supplies from the shed and meet you at your place. We'll make a list of what needs to be done. You can tell Jessie and Trent—when they show up at the studio—about the availability; they have great connections and can help spread the word. And by that point, we should know how close we are to having it ready." *There.* He felt a thousand pounds lighter suddenly.

"Really?" Kira asked through a teary-eyed grin.

"Of course," he assured. "We've got this." Lingering false-alarm chemicals streamed through his system, attempting to further disrupt the peace that was already seeping into him; it would work. Catastrophe avoided. There'd been nothing to panic about after all. What he feared most was Kira having a change of heart. But late payments, finding tenants, and fixing up rentals? Those things Anthony could fix just fine.

He hated that he'd been so quick to crumble. Perhaps he would get better at this having-a-little-faith thing as time went on. He could only hope. After all, if he and Kira were going to make things work, they'd likely face a few bumps in the road.

CHAPTER 14

Kira stepped back to eye the wide arch between the entryway and the front room. Anthony had been right; buying this type of paint was worth the cost. One coat, and the walls in the duplex looked good as new.

With the paint roller still in hand, Kira tugged her phone from the front pocket of her baggy overalls. Nearly seven-thirty and the sun was barely starting to set; they were seeing an end to the dark days of winter at last.

She could hardly believe how much she and Anthony had accomplished since the frightening wake-up call last week. Yet disturbing as it was, that call had sparked a chain of much-needed progress. Thanks to Anthony, who quickly assessed the needs of the rental, they were able to come up with an approximate date that the duplex would be available. A timeframe Kira relayed to Trent and Jessie while taking sweet baby Abby's pictures. Anthony had been right: the Lockhearts were happy to spread the word about the car *and* the duplex, saying the place should be rented in no time. In fact, she already had a showing scheduled for Saturday morning. Even more, a guy from the station put an offer on the car, which—as the tenant suggested—covered the missing rent.

Kira shuffled over the drop-cloth-covered floor, rested the roller at the edge of the paint pan, and climbed onto the window seat. It offered a perfect view of the quiet trail. One that, Kira found, led to the opposite side of the pond she'd dragged Anthony to so many years ago. Country life was beginning to show its draws, and Kira couldn't be more pleased. Still, her attention was drawn to an even more spectacular view. One right there inside the duplex: Anthony.

He stood in the dining area, biceps bulging as he twisted a screwdriver with one hand and supported a chandelier with the other. Kira's heart swelled like the rows of rising rolls she'd seen in the diner. Something that happened only when the recipe was right. The perfect balance of flour and salt, water, and yeast. Even the temperature mattered. And it seemed the more she learned about Anthony, the more he fit that bill of perfection.

She'd often heard the expression *"it's in the little things,"* but Kira hadn't been able to agree. Probably because she hadn't found a guy who had the big things down. But now she understood. Things that were little to him were *huge* to her. Going out to start her car before she went home. Not casting judgment when she shared the broken parts of herself. And being there for her when she needed help.

Her mind drifted to the bigger parts that made Anthony who he was. The man she was quickly falling in love with. He was honest. Hardworking. And cared about the town he lived in. He sought to make it a better place.

Kira couldn't get enough of the pictures she'd taken of him at the diner. It was safe to say she had a dozen favorites, but at the top of that list was the one she'd placed as her laptop screensaver. In it, Anthony stood at the bar, dressed in his kitchen whites, his muscular arms casually spread at either side of the counter. She'd caught him admiring a young family. New parents who fed their young babe his first taste of chocolate shake.

Anthony's expression had said it all. He really *did* want that one day, like he said. And that—that fit into one of the *big* things. Because Kira wanted that, too. And while Cobble Creek was beginning to look like the perfect place to fulfill that life, Anthony was starting to look like the perfect man for it. He was definitely an ideal boyfriend.

The thought took her by surprise. *Was* he her boyfriend?

"Penny for your thoughts, Kira, Kira."

She grinned. Not many people called her that. Mainly her grandparents, in fact. But she liked how it sounded in Anthony's deep, raspy tone. "Um, you really want to know what I'm thinking?" she asked. "It might scare you away."

Anthony, who'd finished hanging the light, had been walking toward her, but at her words he paused and looked up to meet her gaze. There was the look he'd worn the other morning in the diner.

Before she could dissect it further, his expression changed. He dragged a slow step across the drop cloth, a challenge sparking up in his eye. "Try me."

"I know it's only been, like, a month or so, but I was

wondering what we should call this. Like if we're officially dating or ..."

Anthony's brow lifted in what looked like genuine surprise.

Her heart thumped out one beat of regret. "We don't have to call it anything if you don't want to. Like I said, it's early. It's just that since we started dating each other, I haven't felt like dating anyone else." She recalled an incident she had in the store the other day. One she'd purposely *not* told him about, for fear he'd think she was trying to make him jealous. But now seemed like a good time to share it.

"On Tuesday, while I was at the market, some guy ... what was his name—Seth. Yeah. Anyway, he asked me how to tell if a mango is ripe. I showed him, of course, but he kept the conversation going for a while. Asked if I was new here or just passing through."

"Seth Steger," Anthony said through clenched teeth.

Kira felt her eyes widen. "So ... I take it you don't like him?"

"No, I like him. We're friends, actually. And if I hadn't skipped poker night the last few weeks, he'd have known better than to hit on you."

"Hmm," Kira mumbled, biting back a laugh.

"So did he ask you out or what?"

"I think he sensed that I wasn't into the idea, so he left off after saying he'd have to stop by the studio sometime. He wants me to take a look at this old camera he has. Tell him if it's worth anything. Not that I'll know ..."

Anthony hadn't moved so much as a muscle. She surveyed him for a breath; he looked like he'd stepped onto the runway for *Italian Hunk* Magazine. Face fixed in a distant glare. A tight black tee shirt streaked with ashy gray paint, ripped jeans that hung low on his hips, and skin that could force the sunset's glow into a runner-up slot.

"Anyway, this leads back to where we started. If Seth does come into the studio, I *could* always tell him, or anyone else who happens to ask, that I'm dating someone. What do you think?"

❧

Anthony blinked the dryness from his eyes. *What did he think?* This was possibly the most encouraging thing Kira could have said. The idea that she wanted to make something official—before Seth tried to sledgehammer his way into the picture—said she really *was* the commitment type.

He lifted his arms toward her, motioned with his hands for her to come closer.

Kira hung her feet over the ledge of the window seat before sliding off and onto the floor. Her bun had gotten messier throughout the day, and he'd be danged if it didn't add to her beauty. A pair of large overalls hung loosely around her small frame and over a snug tee shirt. She wore fluffy socks again. Today's were gray, which was good, since he'd seen her mop up a few fresh drops of paint from the hardwood floors with them, mainly against the baseboards where the cloth pulled away from the wall.

Mischief danced in those big brown eyes as she stepped over the bunched-up canvas, that pouty lip caught between her teeth. If his heart had settings like a blender, Kira could hit those buttons with a look alone. The particular one she gave him now triggered a setting he hadn't encountered often: *whipped*.

"Well," he said, lifting a hand to her face as she neared. Her cheek, smooth and cool against his palm, flushed pink. "I'm not interested in dating anyone else, Kira. And if you aren't either, then I guess we can make it official." He grinned, let his posture droop like a lazy teen's, and channeled his old high school bravado voice, which sounded a whole lot like Sylvester Stallone's in *Rocky*. "I don't have a ring or nothin' like that, but uh … will you be my girl? I can bring my letterman's jacket to school if you want to wear it."

She grinned, that color in her cheeks deepening. "I would love that." And then, in true Kira fashion, she grabbed his shirt and pulled him in for a kiss.

He was in trouble now. His recent reaction said it all. Just one week ago, Kira had come into the diner with her head hung low, looking as if she were ready to wave that infamous flag. Turned out that wasn't the case, but Anthony had nearly crumbled under pressure. Yet now, as he kissed Kira's warm and tempting lips, Anthony mindfully clambered for that protective guard. The one he used to have poised at the ready. He'd have done anything in that moment to build it high once more. But it was too late.

"Can't believe we're almost done," Kira mumbled against his mouth. "How about we clear out, clean up, then meet back at my place?"

Anthony nodded, took one more kiss before speaking. "Sounds good to me." The phrase *You can't swim if you don't get in the pool* came to mind—something his pop always said. It was fair to say, as Anthony savored the taste of Kira Moretti's mouth once more, that he'd jumped in with both feet. He only prayed he wouldn't regret it.

That train of thought stuck with him as he helped finish the last few details, slowly tugging blue strips of paint-tape from the ceiling and baseboards. The gal who'd moved out had left the duplex in decent condition. Not too much clutter or junk. Thank heavens for that. With a nice layer of paint, the place looked good as new.

As Anthony dragged his supplies back to the truck, Kira hauled the extra paint cans and brushes to the utility garage behind the duplex. While she took a quick shower, Anthony ran home and did the same. She'd invited him back to her place afterward. And though it was getting late, there was no place he'd rather be. Kira had just made a declaration: She wasn't interested in anyone else but him. She was committed to Studio Click and planned to stay right there in the good old town of Cobble Creek.

He'd kissed her earlier, when she said yes about *being his girl.* And as good as that moment had been, he craved more. Craved being close to her without the hesitant voices in his head. Without the reservation that kept those encounters safe in the shallows.

The shops along Main had closed up for the night. All but the bar, a few men climbing off their bikes and heading in. Perhaps if he looked close enough, Anthony would see good ol' Seth. The poor guy was in a similar position. Running a family business, rooted in a place that didn't offer a whole lot of single ladies. Well, Seth would have to keep on looking; Kira was already interested in Anthony.

A warm light glowed from her front window as he pulled into the drive, feeling different from how he'd felt when he left. More confident. He wasn't a fool risking everything for someone who'd take off without warning. He was a man falling in love with a woman. One who planned to stay right there in Cobble Creek.

After a tap on the door, Kira's voice sounded from inside. "Come on in."

Anthony didn't hesitate. Kira sat on the couch, a bottle of lotion nearby as she rubbed both hands down one leg. "Hi," she said. "Come, sit. I'm just letting my hair dry in front of the fire."

He closed the door, glancing at the gas-fueled flames behind the glass. She had her back to it while a fan blew the scent of that lotion throughout the room like a drug. *Her.* It was so her. A scent that reminded him of a rose-colored wine he'd tasted at a recent fundraiser. The tangy sweet scent of wild strawberries.

He plopped onto the other end of the comfy couch, watched as she smoothed her palms over her ankle, and then her foot.

"Thank you so, so much for coming to my rescue this week."

He grinned, a bit of nerves kicking up suddenly. "Any time."

Kira switched her focus to the other leg, squirting another dab of lotion onto her hand before smoothing it over her knee, down the back of her calf. "I can't tell you how much it means to have someone help without acting like I'm a giant mess or a great big burden." She shrugged. "When we talked about my family before, I said I didn't think they were sincere in their compliments. Remember that?"

He nodded, curious. "Yes."

"But after giving it more thought, what I really believe is that they're afraid of me."

He let out a chuckle before realizing she was serious. "Why would they be afraid?"

"They think I'm less predictable than I am. They're all just waiting for me to self-destruct somehow, and *I* keep waiting for them to figure out that that's not going to happen." She rested the lotion on the coffee table and straightened out, draping the bottom half of her legs over his lap, and sighed. "I might mess up here and there. But I'm never as far gone as they think, you know?"

He was guilty of that very thing himself. Misjudging her. Fearing her, even. But he was done with that. Starting tonight, Anthony was all in. He nodded, cupped a hand around one of her knees, and circled his thumb over her silky skin. "I can't speak for your family, but I'll admit to being scared in the beginning."

He risked a glance at her before continuing. "First my mom. Then a couple of women I dated, Ruth and Elsie. Separately—I didn't date them at the same time." Anthony shot her a wink, then shook his head as he continued. "The most important women in my life all left. And when you came in declaring your passion for new adventures, I was terrified. Mainly because I already felt so drawn to you."

Admitting that, with her so close, it dug into a whole new level of vulnerability. Setting his gaze back on her took that connection even further. Deeper. She gulped, lifted her head away from the armrest like she was hanging on the words he spoke.

"But I can truthfully say that I'm not worried anymore. You have it together." He laughed. "I mean, you're going to have stuff sneak up on you, like the due-sooner-than-you-thought house payment. But you've impressed me. You're smart—brilliant. With the way you thought to contact the high school and the ideas you've come up with already. And you're so talented.

Those pictures … wow. I can't get over it." In his excitement, Anthony hadn't noticed the tears welling in Kira's eyes. Not until one trickled down her cheek.

"Really?" she squeaked. "Is that what you see in me?"

The question nearly ripped his heart in half. *Thank you, God, for letting me see this before now.* Before a moment that Kira probably needed more than he'd ever know. "Of course," he said.

At once she was in his arms, her exuberance like the sun itself. A mass of vibrant energy, heat, and light.

In a contortion of arms and legs, the removal of his jacket happening somewhere along the way, they moved onto the floor. A rug as thick and soft as the socks she wore buffered the rigid wood planks beneath. Colorful flames flickered in her eyes as he slipped a hand around the back of her neck. Only this time she didn't rush in and take over like she often did. Instead, Kira stilled, closed her eyes with her face toward his, and sighed.

Anthony looked over her face. Soft, rosy cheeks, hints of moisture caught in her dark lashes, and a vulnerability that sparked a deep admiration. He leaned in and pressed one soft kiss at the corner of her jaw. And then another.

The anticipation was fuel as he moved up her warm cheek, over her brow, and back down the other side of her face. As he neared her delicate earlobe, Kira moaned, kindling an entirely different fire low in his belly. The urgency won out. Anthony rushed in, took her mouth to his in a series of deep, lingering kisses.

She was a taste of heaven. Silky soft, fire hot, and sweeter than anything he'd known. He loved this woman. Cherished her. With the gentle touch of his lips to hers, he admitted that very thing. "I love you, Kira."

Kira pulled back the slightest bit, held his gaze in the low light. "I love you too." She sealed the words with a kiss, and he lingered in every blessed sensation.

Anthony had always hoped to give his heart to someone before he died, even if he *had* been hurt before; he just never imagined giving it to someone so completely. In that moment, Anthony knew his heart belonged more to Kira than it did him.

CHAPTER 15

Kira traced the tip of her finger over her tabletop, spelling out the word *perfect* in big cursive letters. Things had been so perfect last night she could hardly believe it. The more she kissed Anthony, the more she realized just how much a kiss could say about a guy. Python was a greedy kisser. It had always been about him. *Everything* had been about him. Sloppy, hurried kisses with wandering hands. But Anthony ... she sighed. Anthony Marino had mastered the kiss with paced perfection. Slow rapture. And all *the feels* she could hope to feel and more.

I love you, Kira. The words washed over her like liquid sugar. Offering that same, deep-seated thrill every time she replayed them. Which was roughly ninety-nine times that morning. Not to mention the couple of hundred times she'd replayed them before falling asleep.

Anthony Marino loved her. Believed in her. And best of all, as dumb as it sounded, he wasn't afraid of her. Wasn't secretly terrified that she'd up and leave and ruin her own life. His support felt like a rare gift.

Also a gift was the sun as it rose over the east mountain and warmed her back while she checked her to do list. Her new notepad—a gift from Anthony—sported the Tony's Diner logo on top. It made her picture him in the diner, ready to slide a mug of coffee across the bar. She'd sip on it over fresh banter, the conversation more stimulating than the caffeine. Today would be great, she decided while looking over the list. She'd take her laptop to the studio and work on images of the Lockheart's darling baby girl. Talk about adorable. While bundled into a gorgeous wool-knit wrap, Abby had fallen asleep, her tiny face and puckered lips looking doll-like. Another favorite was the one she'd taken on the soft floral mat —a canvas made up of hundreds of pink, silky petals. Kira had tossed a handful of matching petals over the baby to cover her diaper and tucked another into her tiny fist. Kira's heart melted every time she looked at those pictures.

Trent and Jessie had already selected their favorites and ordered a ton of enlargements, prints, and baby announcements—a first for Kira. She could hardly wait to sit down and try out some of the new digital templates she'd bought to create custom cards.

Hopefully she'd book a few more appointments. Maybe get some walk-ins. Anthony had lent her a standing sidewalk sign, which should catch more attention than the marquee. The thing was nearly as tall as she was. She'd pick up some colored chalk at Graham's Pharmacy and write up a special on walk-ins. She planned to switch it up each week or so. This week's offer would include a set of photo mugs with any sitting.

Oh, and she was supposed to show the rental later that night. Yep, things were looking good. Or, as she'd spelled out on the tabletop, perfect. She nodded, giving her to-do list one last glance over, Marissa's visit waving from its designated spot at the bottom, then slipped it into her bag on her way out.

Yet as she neared the car, that pesky little voice told her she was tempting fate. *There's no such thing as perfect. And when Marissa came, she'd see nothing more than a wannabe.* Slim funds coming in. Not many customers to speak of. A woman still trying to find her course in life.

True, she hadn't found her way in life yet. And there wasn't such a thing as perfect. It might take a while to get the duplex rented. Perhaps it'd take months. It could be that the studio would sit empty day after day, and Kira would have to drain her savings and possibly even take out a loan. Maybe that's all Marissa would see when she came next month. But the thing was, none of those things were as important to her as they used to be. Because for the first time in a very long time, Kira didn't have anything to prove. Thanks to Anthony, she felt good enough just the way she was.

CHAPTER 16

Kira blew out a slow, calming breath as she inspected the studio. Three months. *Wow,* she could hardly believe it. Just three months ago she'd started a new chapter in life. And though time had gone by quickly, she'd accomplished more than she imagined was possible. Her planner was peppered with indoor studio sittings, outdoor shoots, upcoming dances, and large events, too. She enjoyed those the most. In fact, last month for Easter, Kira had snapped pictures at Cobble Creek's Easter Egg Hunt. A gal at the community center had hired her to capture some of the goings-on that day, along with staged portraits with the Easter Bunny. It'd been a blast. But still, one thing Kira was most proud of was the graffiti wall she'd come up with for senior portraits. Prior to their scheduled appointments, graduates of Cobble Creek High were invited to come and personalize part of the studio's brick wall by spray-painting a background that represented them—perfect for teens. Luckily, Hammers Hardware carried plenty of washable spray paint for the occasion.

Another hit was her newly finished kids' corner—a spot Anthony helped her create for the little ones. While small visitors sat up to the table for a tea party in the charming, miniature kitchen, Kira snapped away. Sisters giggling over tiny teacups, laced gloves accentuated lifted pinkies while knitted shawls hung over their small frames. Adjacent to the kitchen, mock tools dangled from small brass hooks on an old-time pegboard. Greasy coveralls draped over rusty-looking nails, ready for the next "mechanic" to work on the knickknacks on the workbench. A tiny tots library separated the two opposing scenes, offering a spot where kids could cuddle up to mom or dad, big sis or bro, and giggle at the selection of classic picture books. All of this while Kira captured the moments.

Business was good, and she'd never felt so accomplished in her life. But Kira wasn't sure it would be enough to impress her older sister who, over time, had proven to be one of her toughest critics. And what would she say to Mom and Dad about the visit? *Sure, Kira's doing good now, but we all know it's not going to last. Give her time, and she'll mess it up like she does everything else.*

Kira hated setting such low expectations for Marissa. It wasn't fair, and she knew it. Perhaps this visit could mark a new beginning for them both.

A ding sounded from her phone just as she thought to check the time. It was from Anthony. Speaking of good. *Wonderful* was more like it. She peered down at his text:

. . .

What time does your sister get here?

Kira straightened up and turned to look over her shoulder. If she squinted hard enough, looking beyond passersby on Main Street, she could possibly make out his impressive stature behind the bar. Or at least imagine seeing him between Chuck and Don as they ate their Saturday morning special. Her phone let out another ding.

Are you sure you don't want me to come to the airport? I will, you know.

Yes, bless him. But no, this was something she had to do herself. Besides, Anthony would meet Marissa soon enough.

I do know that. Thank you for offering, but I've got this. I'll be over in a minute to kiss you goodbye.

It dinged back in a hurry.

Mmm ... Can't wait. Let's kiss hello too. Then goodbye. I like it better when we do that.

. . .

She chuckled, bathing in the thrill that bubbled up in her chest. She and Anthony were in the honeymoon phase of a relationship. The hate-being-apart, want-to-go-everywhere-together, make-a-special-trip-to-say-goodbye phase. And Kira was loving every minute of it. Which had made last night difficult; with the weather turning warm so quickly, Shadow River had risen too high, causing flooding along the edge of town. Rather than spending a nice quiet evening together like they'd planned, Anthony had gone off to help sandbag the fire station.

Today's three-hour trip to the Jackson Hole Airport, when doubled, would take up most of the day. Which meant she wouldn't see much of him today either. No early lunch before the studio opened. No quick visits between sittings. But Marissa had taken time out of her life to visit her—a visit Kira had cleared her schedule for once her sister confirmed the dates—it'd be worth it.

Sunlight poured over Main Street as Kira locked up the storefront. Cobble Creek hadn't seen snow since the first of April, and Kira had finally unpacked her shorts and capris. She'd also tucked her winter coats away for the season, needing only an occasional jacket or raincoat. She paused to take in the magic of the quaint, side-by-side shops. One walk down Main offered townsfolk places like CC's Salon, Top's Bakery, and the Flower Girl Floral Shop. Kira's new favorites were Books and Nooks, Frank and Signs, and of course the Old-Fashioned Soda Shop in the pharmacy. Baskets of fresh produce lined the storefront just a few doors from Tony's Diner, the color as vibrant and diverse as the people she'd met. This was truly the place Kira belonged, and that knowledge meant more to her than she could say.

Kira intended to listen to an audiobook during the drive to the airport, but by the time she remembered that idea, she was more than halfway there. Her mind preoccupied with a mixing pot of memories. She and Marissa when they were young. Many put a smile on her face. Some were tender enough to make her cry. Others had Kira shaking her head, wondering why her older sister had often been so harsh.

When she'd stepped over to the diner to tell Anthony goodbye, he'd offered some encouraging words, assuring her there was no reason to dread the visit. "Your family loves you," he assured. "And they want to see you succeed." The best part about Anthony was that he never made her feel like she'd be less great without him. He simply had a way of helping Kira see her strengths—qualities that existed with or without him. She wasn't sure why that felt so important to her, but it did.

The sun shone in full force as Kira took the turn into the airport. Just the sight of the tarmac from a distance, the planes coming and going overhead, all of it caused an odd sort of cabin pressure to build right there in her compact car. Anthony had shown her how to use a pressure cooker just last week. He'd pointed out the dos and don'ts. Explained how the contraption needed time to build, and then release pressure with each use, which made Kira relate to the thing on some level. It was very *human* to build pressure over time. Most explosive outbursts were layered with mounds of pressure. Layers that had built up over years. And then, with the simplest trigger, it could go off.

Kira gripped the steering wheel and forced out a pursed-lipped breath. She didn't have steam to let off, did she? She didn't think so. Kira had finally found the happiness she was looking for. The place she belonged whether her family believed she'd stay put or not. And that's what mattered most.

After locking up the car, Kira weaved through the lot. This section of parking was covered, and the lack of sunlight made it feel like winter had made a sudden comeback. She folded her arms over her chest as she scanned the exit gate. *Calm, Kira. Calm. Things will be great.*

❧

"Burger, deep-fried mushrooms, and a root beer," Anthony said as he slid Sheriff Trent Lockheart's lunch across the counter. "Can I get you anything else?"

Trent shook his head. "No, looks great. Hey, I can't thank you enough for all your help last night. According to Judy, the fire station suffered leaks in years past, but nothing so severe."

Anthony covered a yawn. "I was happy to help. Never know how much damage a runoff like that can cause."

"I'll say," Benny said around a mouth of food. He nudged the sheriff. "That's what I was telling Trent. We had one heck of a winter. And when things heat up quick, we can end up with a big mess."

Trent dabbed his mouth with a napkin. "Glad the majority of town sits outside the danger zone," he said, lifting his drink to where the straw waited an inch from his lips. "Better to have the fire station at risk than the health clinic, or someone's home or personal business."

Anthony nodded. "True enough. And we've got one heck of a community. That's what I love about this place."

"Hear, hear," Benny cheered, lifting his cup of root beer with a stretched out arm.

Anthony secured a fresh glass from under the counter to play along, straightening his arm to clank it against the officers'. "Hear, hear." He brought the empty glass to his lips and tipped it back, way back, before placing it solidly on the counter. "Good stuff."

"Hey," Benny said. "Since the ladies are getting together for book club tonight, some of us are heading out for some bowling if you want to come."

Anthony tilted his head as he weighed the option. "Thanks. If Kira takes longer than she plans, I might just take you up on that."

He gave the two a nod before slipping out of the serving area and striding down the hall toward his office. He lowered himself onto the wheeled chair and stewed. Talking with Sheriff Lockheart and Benny Gains had triggered something: a spot of discomfort that was spreading dangerously fast. *The flood.* The fact that something as innocent and natural as melting snow could cause a lot of damage under the right (or wrong) circumstance. The very idea crawled into his brain like a tick. Sneaky at first. Hardly even recognized. But boy, could it cause a lot of trouble if it wasn't snuffed out.

For Anthony, it was fear. Fear that having Kira's sister in town might trigger those old feelings of inadequacy. That impulse to prove herself to her family. Which could result in her picking up and leaving.

The first spot of fear surfaced as Kira walked out of the diner that morning after kissing him goodbye. He couldn't scratch the image. Suddenly it was his mom, then Ruth, then Elsie, each walking thoroughly out of his life. Never to return.

Anthony pounded a fist against his desk. *"Enough,"* he grumbled, kicking the small trashcan by his feet. He told Kira he wouldn't fear her. That he *didn't* fear her. Besides, this had more to do with Anthony than it did Kira Moretti. Perhaps what he needed was a good counseling session or two. Clear his head of the issues he'd faced since his mother left.

He knew Kira was only gone for a few hours, but a sudden loneliness kicked in. He remembered the way his dad changed after his diagnoses. He'd tendered up real quick after that. And he made a habit of asking Anthony for something he needed in increased doses as he went through treatments: hugs. Wordlessly, the man would nod to him, lift his arms, and look at him expectantly.

Anthony would respond gladly, needing the closeness as well. The longest embrace they shared was after they discovered he wasn't responding to the treatments as they'd hoped. And that—at best—he had another two months to live. On that day Dad didn't have to ask. He'd simply looked at Anthony after the doctor gave them time to discuss their limited options. The slightest nod and Anthony was there. Glad that the big, strong man had it in him to show that he needed it. He remembered wondering who'd be there to embrace him once Dad was gone.

That's when the book club stepped into action. Run by a couple ladies from the church on Steeple Street, one being the pastor's wife, the collection of woman swooped in with casseroles, books on grieving, framed inspirational quotes, and plenty of hugs to go with each thoughtful delivery. The fine community of Cobble Creek at its best. Thank the good Lord for it. Anthony did just that every day.

The more recent gratitude at his lips was centered around Kira. Daily he lifted thanks for her and vowed he'd do right by her the best he could. He put his mind in that mode and rolled his chair back enough to hoist his feet onto his desk. Hunkering deeper into the comfortable office chair, Anthony leaned his head back and closed his eyes, ready to catch up on some much-needed rest after the flood. And hoping to avoid disaster of a whole different kind.

CHAPTER 17

Kira's family always said she stood out in a crowd. Loud. Boisterous. Sure to be seen and heard. In school, that might have been true. But who wanted to go unnoticed among their high school class? She *had* stood out. Gained popularity for a number of things: *Biggest Flirt. Cutest Brunette.* And Kira's personal favorite, *Most Likely to Make You Spit Out Your Milk* (the yearbook staff's version of funniest guy or girl).

Meanwhile, Marissa—her complete opposite—was never on the radar for stuff like that. The girl got straight and still wasn't voted by her classmates as *brainiest babe* because she made it her job in life to blend. The thing was, had her older sister been some wild, rebellious child, Kira would've looked like the tame one. It was all relative.

Still, as Kira scanned the crowd, considering her sister's aversion to standing out, she spotted her among the moving heads with ease. People usually slouched as they sat or walked or stood. At least a little. Marissa didn't. And her love for turtlenecks and layered clothes surfaced anytime she stepped out of the state of Nevada. As if the world were divided into two distinct areas: Nevada and Iceland.

And there she was, back rod-straight, a bag in each fist as she strode, looking composed amongst a sea of chaotic bustling. Folks tapping at phone screens, scrambling for items in bags and backpacks, or chugging down bottles of water. Marissa, for all her work to go unnoticed over the years, stood out in a crowd after all, and Kira couldn't help but be charmed by it.

She grinned wide when their eyes met, her nerves all but gone. A rush of love and adoration poured into her at the sight of her sister. She scurried toward Marissa, rushing around a pillar, only to bump into the trash bin hiding behind it. Kira moved on, ducking beneath a retractable line barrier, and hurried over to give Marissa an exuberant hug.

"Why didn't you just wait until the end of the gate like everyone else?" Marissa grumbled, pointing to a crowd filtering through the gate's exit.

Kira only grinned. "I'm so glad you're here." And she meant it, for the most part. "Let me take these." Kira pried a small carry-on case from one hand and an oversized bag from the other. "Did you check luggage or is this it?"

Marissa readjusted the purse strap hanging over her shoulder. "Just carry-on," she said, turning to look behind her.

"Well, are you hungry? Want to stop and get something to eat or just head right to my place? We can go to the diner and grab food once we get there if you'd like. Or they have this amazing little produce stand where they serve up fresh veggies with jicama, sweet peppers, all the fancy stuff you like …" Kira died off there as she realized Marissa was looking over her shoulder once more. Gawking was more like it.

"Is there someone you want to talk to?" Kira asked, wondering if her sister had met someone during the flight.

"Well," Marissa said, her brown eyes tight as she searched, "I have a surprise for you." She checked the gold watch at her wrist and muttered to herself. "Where are they?"

They?

Mom and Dad—her parents must've come too. Kira's heart thundered as she turned to scan the passengers filtering out of the gate. She'd spoken with her parents about a dozen times or so since moving to Cobble Creek and texted more often than that. She'd sent pictures of the studio, outdoor snapshots of Main Street. Things between them were good. But they'd never hinted they might join Marissa for the trip there.

A new wave of emotion took over as she considered seeing her parents now too. But then she saw something she hadn't—for the life of her—expected to see. She thumped Marissa with her elbow. "Do *you* see who *I* see, or am I going crazy?" Monty—skinny, cocky, and tall—slithered along the outskirts of the crowd.

"*That's* who I was looking for."

"*What!*" If dumbfounded was an emotion, it had taken over every possible feeling she could feel. "But you said *they*. Like *two people* they."

"Yeah, see?" Marissa tipped her head in Monty's direction. Kira jerked her eyes back to the crowd, barely able to get over the sight of her ex-boyfriend, when she spotted Finny Shea. "What is *happening*?" She hadn't believed in such things as mortal enemies before, but in that moment those two fit the bill for Kira. And her sister had carted them all the way to her new place?

"Don't be mad at me," Marissa said, stretching out the final word in a patronizing tone. "Python and Finny have a lot to talk to you about, and they insisted on doing that in person. In fact …" Marissa leaned in. "They're the ones who paid for my flight here."

This had all just gotten way too weird. Kira had had plenty of dreams that didn't make sense. Driving down a winding road in a Ferrari one moment only to open a beeping microwave the next. All so she could settle into a cloud that turned into a giant purple swimming pool. This—seeing Monty and Finny Shea in the Wyoming airport, having come with her sister, no less—was crazy-dream bizarre. Kira had to pause and consider whether or not she'd really gotten out of bed that morning.

Marissa's thin, waving arm was a silent siren, causing every sort of alarm to call out in Kira's head. *Gather the troops. We've got trouble heading our way.* Still, she stood there, stunned-faced and bug-eyed, staring in horror as the odd, eccentric duo strutted toward her.

"Just go with it," Marissa mumbled. "You'll find out why they're here soon enough."

"Kira," Monty called, tossing one arm around her. She knew hugs were supposed to be two-sided, but among the stiff denim of his jacket and the fresh shock from his presence, Kira couldn't move. Finny came in for a one-armed hug next. Layers of white feathery fluff coated Finny's scrawny frame, making her feel birdlike as Kira managed a pat to her back.

"Thank you for letting us crash your party, dear," Finny cooed in her thick Swedish accent. "We'll let you have some time with your sister while we get caught up on rest—jet lag, you know. How about we meet up at, say, eight o'clock?"

"That'd be perfect," Marissa blurted.

If Kira didn't know better, she'd say her sister was star-struck—which was annoying, considering what the two had done to Kira.

They toted off then, luggage dragging behind them as they headed toward the exit.

"Don't worry," Marissa said. "They have their own rental car. They're planning to stay at the Country Quilt Inn, so you won't have to put them up or anything."

Kira turned to her sister. "Okay, time to speak up. What is going on?"

"So those guys came in on the same flight as you?" Kira floored the pedal in her small car as it puttered up to speed.

"No, they came in straight from L.A. on Finny's private jet," Marissa said. "I just told them when I was flying in so they could come at the same time."

"I would literally rather die than talk to either one of those guys," Kira said.

"Would you *please* avoid using the word *literal* in a *non-literal* sense? I'm around middle school kids all day, for crying out loud."

Kira wasn't so sure it *wasn't* in the literal sense. "I have nothing to say to those clowns. Why are they even here?"

Marissa leaned her head deeply to one side, speaking as she rolled forward and tipped it the other way in a neck stretch.

"They don't want me to tell you, so I'm not telling you. You'll find out as soon as we meet up with them."

"This is … I was hoping to just have some time with my sister, you know? Show you around the studio and the town, introduce you to some people …"

"Like your new *boyfriend*?" Marissa asked it like she was talking to a young student. One whose romance could only fit into some silly world of pretend.

"Yes," Kira said with a sigh. She swallowed hard and squeezed the steering wheel, wishing she could clench the chaos in her stomach before it spread over her entire body. "Listen, Marissa. We all have pieces of our past that, like, sting." She paused there, wondering briefly if her sister would relate. "Python and Finny are the worst piece of my past. People I'd be happy to go my entire life without seeing ever again. So having this—whatever it is—sprung on me like this is my worst nightmare."

"No, not your *worst* nightmare. I'm sure that would be something a little more intense. Like burning to death. Watching your loved ones burn to death. Why does this generation have to exaggerate so much?"

"Marissa?" Kira snapped. "Could you just be *human* for a minute? I'm not one of your students, and unless you've miraculously aged a hundred years, you and I are from the same generation, so just knock it off."

Marissa cleared her throat and turned her head toward the scenery out her window. They were on the freeway now, surrounded by blue sky, the occasional field of growing green, and a whole lot of roaming cattle.

Kira took the next twenty minutes to organize her thoughts.

Things she could say that wouldn't sound spiteful or angry and above all—dramatic. "I think it's fair to say most people don't want to run into their ex-boyfriends. Do you agree?" She glanced over in time to see Marissa nod. A big, appreciative nod. *Good.* "Especially if things ended badly. Which in this case —they did. Very badly."

"True," Marissa agreed again. Perhaps this wouldn't be as bad as Kira feared. At least the getting-through-to-her-sister part.

"And to make the situation worse, the woman who represents a huge part of that pain—the *uber*-successful fashion designer who believed *him* over *me*—is here too. Basically, the pair represents a period of my life that I'd rather forget ever happened. And so when you add to that the fact that your only sister arranged the entire thing without even consulting you, it's a lot to take in."

"That makes sense," Marissa said with another nod.

Either her sister had shifted from teaching to counseling at the middle school, or she'd learned to diffuse Kira's anger over the years.

"I would never set you up to get hurt, Kira," Marissa said. "I'm actually trying to make up for being kind of a crummy sister lately."

Kira lifted a brow.

Marissa smiled. "I don't want to give you all the details because I told them I wouldn't, but the reason I allowed this is because I think you'll be very happy with what they're offering. Part of which is a chance to clear up the Moretti name, along with an apology—which I think is long overdue."

Those last few words were antacids to the burning in her heart. "You do?"

Marissa shot her a surprised look. "Of *course* I do. The whole family wants that for you."

Kira nodded, needing that tidbit more than she knew. "That's nice to hear, actually."

"I don't know why you're surprised. We all just want what's best for you."

"Thanks," Kira said with a grin. "I know. Of *course*." She wasn't sure why she felt the need to tack on that last part. Perhaps Kira was assuring them both that she knew that much. Her family wanted nothing less than the best for her. *That* had never been the issue. Determining whether or not she could obtain what was best—or even identify it—was the real issue.

She thought back on the awkward greeting at the airport. *Ugh*. Kira was making a name for herself out there, and she hated the idea of two detached-from-reality egomaniacs waltzing in and ruining it. In all fairness, Kira had no right to call Finny Shea names. The woman was eccentric, sure, but she'd never been mean. Just wrong about whom she believed in the whole stolen images scandal. And who could blame her for believing the snake, since she was falling in love with him?

At least she would finally put this behind her. With any luck, the pair would be gone by tomorrow, and Kira could get on with her life. Now she just had to update Anthony with the limited details she had. She was already dreading it.

CHAPTER 18

Anthony stared down the glossy lane to the white pins beneath the lights. He channeled all the frustration raging through him, then rushed in to unleash the ball. The sixteen-pounder let out a low growl as it spun over the polished wood like a panther in pursuit. In one fast explosion, the pins scattered, creating a deceiving show; once the dust cleared, the ball sinking into the machine's gullet, two pins remained—the pin far on the left and the opposite pin at the far right.

"You threw it too hard," Benny said before tipping back a bottle of beer.

"Yeah," Seth shook his head. "You're going to have to ease up on that ball if you want to catch up."

"Go easy on him, guys," Trent said. "He hasn't had a guys' night in a while. He'll get his groove back."

Anthony spotted the gray ball as it shot from the retriever and back onto the rack. He reached down, secured it in his grip, and tried very hard not to think about what an ex-boyfriend would want from his ex-girlfriend who'd not only moved on with her life, but did so in an entirely different state.

He stepped up to an imaginary line and glared at the pins. Should he go for the left and hope to knock out the right with the spinning pin? He could try. He focused hard, swung back, and set his eyes on the left. No, maybe the one on the right. But it was too late; the ball was already on its way, barreling dead center down the lane.

Nothing but air. Not good.

The guys groaned in the background. Benny tapped him on the back and pressed a cold bottle into his hand. "Here," he said. "Looks like you need this."

The truth was, Anthony didn't know what he needed. "Thanks." He shuffled back to the bench and sank into the chair beside Seth.

"You all right, man?" Seth asked.

Anthony nodded. "Yeah, I just … have to get my mind off Kira right now. Her stupid ex flew into town, and she's meeting up with him tonight."

"Whoa," Seth said. "That doesn't sound good at all."

"I know. Apparently the ex brought his girlfriend with him, and they both want to talk to her."

"That just got weird," Logan said under his breath.

"Tell me about it." The situation was putting him to the test; he couldn't deny it. "The funny thing is," Anthony said, "Kira told me I could come if I wanted."

Seth's eyes doubled in size. "You're kidding me. Why aren't you there?" The guys' loud reaction gained attention from the others.

"Why ain't he where?" Benny, who'd just tossed a gutter ball, strode closer.

Anthony looked over to see if Seth wanted to explain, before opting to do it himself. "Kira called me when she and her sister got back from the airport, but added that she had gotten an *un*pleasant surprise. Her ex-boyfriend and his new girlfriend flew in with her sister, and they're staying at the bed and breakfast."

Trent perked up. "Want me to have someone put sand in their sheets?"

Benny smacked him in the stomach. "Jessie would never let you do that."

Trent sneered. "It was a *joke*. When have I ever done a thing like that?"

"Let him finish," Seth said. "This is better than one of those dysfunctional talk shows."

Anthony rolled his eyes. "These two seriously wronged Kira a few years ago by stealing some images she shot at a fashion show in Milan, and when Kira tried to sue them, they dragged her family's name through the mud. It was devastating. According to her sister, they want to make it right." He glanced away from the group, set his gaze on a lane where an entire set of pins got knocked down by the sweeping cleanup bar. The messy heap was shoved out of sight, and then a shiny new set took its place. Ten white pins standing tall. The others forgotten like yesterday's news.

"You're leaving out the best part," Seth griped. "Kira said he could be there when they talked, and instead he's here with us."

A few quiet groans and hums sounded over the guys.

Anthony picked the married men of the bunch to set his focus on; they knew women better than the rest of them.

Benny shook his head. "Shoulda gone. If a woman says you can *go* somewhere but then gives you a choice, the correct choice goes as follows." He passed his beer to Seth and got both hands involved. "If *she's* going to the place she said you can go, then she wants you to go, too."

"Yep," a few mumbled in the background.

"But," Benny continued, "if she *isn't* going to the place she says you can go, then she secretly wants you to *stay*. There. With her." Benny looked at Trent for backup while snatching his bottle back from Seth.

Trent tipped his head from one side to the next, lips tight as he weighed Benny's words. "That's about right."

"Great," Anthony said. "Guess I screwed up."

"No no no, don't worry." Benny motioned for Seth to move, then hunkered into his seat, throwing an arm around him and leaning in. "We *all* make those mistakes. How do you think we know this stuff? Not because they *tell* us. But because they *train* us. You see?"

No. No, he did *not* see. "Yeah," he said with a nod. "Thanks."

Benny tipped his drink toward him. "Any time."

CHAPTER 19

"Why did we agree to meet them in a *bar?"* Kira griped as she watched the door.

Marissa was a butterfly in a beehive. Too soft and frilly for the hard edges of crude language, clanking glass, and heavy music that was more felt than heard. And not metaphorically, either. When the band was in full swing, the rumble caused the shot glasses along the counter to bounce and hum.

"I don't mind it," Marissa lied. She lifted her glass of iced seltzer water with a wedge of lemon and a slice of lime and brought the double red straws to her lips. "Mmm …"

Kira fought back an eye roll and turned to look at the entrance.

"Hey, Kira?"

"Yeah," she replied, eyes still set on the doorway.

"I'm sorry for not having your back the way I should have," Marissa said, leaning in and practically belting the words.

Kira tipped back, held her sister's gaze for a moment.

"I always knew Monty stole your images, but I told myself you deserved it. You didn't, but …" She sighed, her shoulders dropping as she slid her drink closer.

"But *what*?" Kira asked.

Marissa poked at the citrus wedges with her straws. One after the next. "I envied you for being so … quick to do things most people were too scared to do—things *I'd* be too scared to do. I told myself you were irresponsible, but then you came out here and did all these amazing things with the studio." She shrugged. "Mom and Dad have been showing me the texts. And I realized that more often than not, you were brave. You've always known how to *live* life, you know? Even when risk is involved."

Wow. Kira could hardly believe her ears. "Marissa," she said, choked with an onslaught of emotion. "Thank—"

"Oh," Marissa hissed with a nod. "They're here. We'll talk more later."

Kira spun to see the couple striding into the place like the party had arrived. Finny whipped her white, hip-length hair over one shoulder with the exaggerated sway of her long, giraffe-like neck. The woman had a list of unique features that only made her more beautiful. Exotic. After all, Finny Shea started out as a model before she designed her own clothing line and ran her namesake magazine. Most didn't achieve a fraction of what she'd accomplished after living ninety-plus years, but that didn't stop the determined thirty-year-old.

Kira hated to admit it, but Monty looked like a rock star. A sloppy, stayed-up-partying-all-night rock star, but one nonetheless. He swaggered through wafting smoke as flashing lights bounced off his sunglasses. He'd gotten more ink on his neck, a reptilian pattern he'd started on his chest while Kira was dating him. How she'd managed to ever find him attractive, she couldn't say. He might have a magnetic appeal on the surface, but lots of dangerous things did. Including the snake he related himself to. After all, how perilous could a nonvenomous snake be?

Of course, Kira had discovered for herself that there was more than one way to hurt a person. And the truth was, as she watched necks wrench and heads turn, she was still reeling from the effects of it all. She'd been *so close* to being someone. To impressing the likes of Finny Shea, her designing crew, and a handful of A-list models in the least of it. More than that, she'd have made her family proud.

Kira straightened as they neared, patted her hair to assure it was in place, and lifted her chin. Perhaps she should have paid more attention when she'd gotten ready. Or when she touched up her makeup before coming. Finny's pale skin glowed like she'd doused it with a million tiny sparkles.

Marissa shot to her feet and extended a hand across the table. "Hey, guys," she hollered.

Finny, always the professional, shook her hand before reaching for Kira's. Her eyes were lavender today—no surprise; she had a new color for every outfit. "Miss Moretti. Thank you for taking the time to meet with us. It's very gracious of you."

"Hope you don't mind meeting us outside of that rinky-dink town," Monty said. Kira had always envied Finny's Swedish accent. Obviously Monty had too, because he'd adapted one of his own. "The bar in Cobble Creek only lets locals take the stage. We were hoping for a little more than hicks strumming banjos and thumping coffee cans."

The couple broke into laughter. Even Marissa joined in. Kira only stared at them and cleared her throat.

"Anyway, we're not here to make fun of your new life, Kira," Monty assured with his phony accent. "We're here to make you an offer."

Finny piped up, leaning across the table, her flawless face calm. "Marissa graciously agreed to arrange this so that we could *both* apologize. Upon seeing your work years ago, I knew I wanted *you* to shoot in Milan. And after you accepted—and did a stellar job of it, I might add—I repaid you by calling you a liar and letting you go."

Finny gave Monty a nod. "Python here had me fooled at first. Or perhaps I wasn't fooled at all. Perhaps I only *wanted* to believe him. But I discovered the truth soon enough."

"Soon enough to admit it in court?" Kira asked. Forget the shot glasses bouncing to the beat. Her heart was hammering a clash of drums and cymbals.

Monty and Finny looked at each other. "I was still denying it, Kira," he admitted.

"That's true," Finny said, "but I knew better. You can't *fake* taking photographs like the ones you captured, Kira." Finny motioned to a waitress passing by, ordered two virgin drinks Kira had never heard of, then stretched her long, slender arms across the table.

Kira looked down at them, white against the dark wood, wondering what Finny wanted her to do. Place her hands on there, too, so she could hold them while she spoke? No thanks.

"You have a gift, Kira. Something years of training won't touch. And we want you back."

The *we* part in that sentence threw her off. Marissa must have sensed that, because she tapped Kira's shoulder.

"Python's Finny's partner now. Business partner."

Monty gave her a *soak-in-that* look while Kira's jaw clenched. "What do *you* bring to the table?" she couldn't help but ask. Last she looked, *dumb and broke* weren't the best traits one could offer an already successful business owner.

"The charm," Finny said. "People love him."

"Not *all* people," Kira corrected with a glare.

"Hey, I said I'm sorry for doing that, okay? That's why I'm here. To make it right." His accent was gone. "I regret saying that those pictures were mine."

Kira stared at the look on Monty's face as he popped a cigarette in his mouth and lit it. "*And* you abandoned me," she said. "Left me stranded and fending for myself in a foreign country. And then you *lied* about it in court. I didn't get paid for the shoot. I didn't even get reimbursed for my flight." She turned her attention back to Finny. "The least you could've done is give me what I was asking for in court. Not make me look like a fool for suing such a big name."

"You're right," she said. "I feel so horrible about wronging you. I cannot tell you how awful it makes us feel." She and Monty shot one another a glance before Monty gave her a nod. "We're going through a rehab program."

Rehab? Kira was stunned.

"We'd appreciate it if you allowed us to make amends. If you agree to shoot at out next fashion show, I'll not only pay you twice what I pay other photographers, I'll give you everything I owe you and add twelve percent interest to it."

Marissa shifted in her seat. "Kira, you can't pass up this opportunity. There's no way."

She thought about the publicity the case received. "Would you guys do something to clear my name? Like contact the press and explain what happened?"

Finny thanked the waitress as she brought their drinks then leaned over the table once more. "The six major networks, yes. And we'll also clear your name with the agencies who caught wind of things and explain that there was a critical error in the processing department, but that it's since been discovered and made right."

Kira lifted a brow. "Critical error?"

"Python is a partner in Finny Shea," the woman explained. "We couldn't likely smear his name and build our line at the same time."

"That's true," Finny said. "I tried to think of a way to reimburse you without strings attached—that being committing to the upcoming shoot—but for both legal and tax reasons, I can't."

Excitement started like a tiny blizzard in Kira's chest, whirling and growing until it gripped hold of her every limb. Making it feel like she'd entered a walk-in freezer suddenly. It's what happened when Kira was about to do something life-altering. She couldn't believe she was even considering it. But to clear the Moretti name once and for all … she couldn't turn a chance like that down. "When's the fashion show?"

"In five days," Monty said.

"*What?* Oh my gosh. There's no way I could make that work."

"But if you come with us," Finny added, "we'd need to leave tomorrow evening on the private jet."

Kira shot her sister a look. "What about Marissa? She just got here."

"We'll pay for her to come back after your return, since we hijacked her visit this time," Finny said.

"And when would I be back? Like, a week or something?"

"We'd need you to commit to the entire tour. First New York, then Paris, Milan, with the last stop in Barcelona. You'd be back in about forty-five days."

"No." Kira shook her head. "Sorry, no. I just started my life here. I'm really happy."

"Running your grandpa's little studio, Kira?" Monty blurted. "Come on. You *know* small-town life doesn't suit you. It's the reason you left the first time."

"He's right," Finny said. "If you stayed on with us, which we're willing to entertain after this run, you'd be paid generously and enjoy the life of a high-profile photographer in the industry. This could be the start of a very promising career."

"Or ..." Marissa said, "she could do the forty-five-day tour and come home."

Home. Marissa had called Cobble Creek Kira's home.

"Correct," Finny said. "We already have the papers drawn up in an offer. You're welcome to have a lawyer look over it, but we need you to sign before flying out."

Wow. This was really happening. Kira slumped back in her seat. She wasn't even *considering* the last part, of course—starting a career outside of Cobble Creek; she'd never want a life without Anthony. The mere thought of him caused the ache and upset to collide anew. "I might consider the forty-five days," she said softly. "But that's it. I really love it here." She shot Monty a look. "And that studio is the best gift anyone's given me."

Monty took a deep drag, then blew a cloud of smoke toward her face. "You better make up your mind quick, Kira. Our departure time isn't going to budge."

Finny reached into a flat, glitter-covered bag, pulled out a manila folder, and handed it to Kira. "Choose wisely, Ms. Moretti." She reached for her drink, her long delicate fingers gracefully curling around the glass, and turned her face toward the band on stage.

The action said *you're dismissed* like she'd spoken it aloud.

Marissa scooted out of the booth and came to a stand. Kira did the same, the folder in her hand growing heavier with each breath. As they shuffled toward the exit, Finny's offer hung heavy in the air, thicker than the light-trapping haze. She wanted to talk to Marissa now that things were finally on the table; figure out why she'd agreed to help set this up. More than that, she *had* to talk to Anthony. That thought alone had Kira hashing over the dilemma all the way to the car.

"So are we going to discuss this?" Marissa asked as Kira steered the compact car out of the lot.

"In a minute," she said, needing to gather her thoughts first. She glanced at the speed limit sign as they passed, wanting very badly to go twice the speed. She resisted. Only gripped the wheel and wondered why this had to come up in her life right then. *Why,* when she clearly couldn't accept it, did something as wonderful as that offer have to be thrown in her face?

"You're being pretty quiet over there," Marissa said.

"I know. I'm sorry." Kira peered at the lane markings as she approached a sharp curve up ahead. Watched as it shifted from a single yellow dash to two solid lines. Lines that showed where she should and *shouldn't* go. "I just ... can't imagine saying yes to that." She sniffed. "But I can't imagine saying no either."

"You *shouldn't* say no, Kira. You'd be crazy to."

Kira shook her head as more frustrated tears welled in her eyes. "You don't understand."

"Then tell me why you can't go. *You're* the brave one, remember?"

More curves lay up ahead, those solid double lines in sharp focus beneath the beam's glow. "Because I'm not like everyone else. I do stupid stuff and mess things up. I'll probably ruin my shot with Anthony. If I leave, he'll ..." She paused there, the panicky ache sinking deeper into her chest. "Anthony's been through a lot in his life. Enough that even mentioning the offer might set him into a tailspin."

"Mom and Dad will be disappointed if you don't take it."

Kira shot her a look. "They already *know* about it?"

"*Everyone* does. Aunt Leonna, Aunt Tullie, Aunt—"

"You know," Kira blurted, shaking her head, "I'm sick of trying to predict what will impress everyone. I don't care anymore." A fresh wave of guilt swept in, reminding Kira that her sister had apologized mere moments ago. That was all well and good, but it didn't make her decision any easier.

"If Anthony loves you, he'll understand," Marissa said.

Quiet crept into the car. A suffocating blackness that made her want to scream aloud just to prove that she could. Instead, she reached over and gave the radio knob a push with her fist. A loud, angst-filled song blasted from the speakers, satisfying the part of Kira that felt like a trapped animal.

She fixed her eyes on the dark road. Her side of the lane. Her side of the lane. She needed to just stay on her side of the lane. Forget about clearing the family's name. For once, Kira needed to do the safe thing. Even if she *would* regret letting the opportunity pass.

CHAPTER 20

Anthony stared at the lampshade in the front room as he heard Kira pull into his driveway. The car door slammed shut, but no footsteps sounded. He tilted his head to better listen as a knock tapped at the door.

"Come in," he said cautiously. This was how he felt when he'd gone in to hear his father's diagnosis. And then his prognosis. Terrified, exhausted, and ill to the core. Kira's phone call had put him there in an instant. She'd sounded so frantic. So… broken, it was hard *not* to know what she might say.

The screen door creaked as she pulled it open and stepped in, one puffy sock-covered foot at a time. Which explained the lack of footfalls outside. His gaze moved up the length of her. Baggy sweats. A worn tee shirt. Red-rimmed eyes and blotchy cheeks. "Hi," she said, in a hoarse voice.

He'd planned to stay in place. Sit on the lounge chair while Kira said what she had to say. But as soon as their eyes met, the weight of her dilemma, whatever it was, sank into his heart like a millstone.

Anthony shot to a stand and crossed the floor, wrapping his arms solidly around her.

"I needed this so bad." Her warm, tiny frame jerked and heaved as she fought for the words. "I never want to leave you, Anthony. Ever."

He clenched his eyes shut, took in those wonderful words, and sighed. "That's good," he mumbled. "Because I never *want* you to leave." He ran his jaw along the side of her face. And while her skin was flushed and hot, the tears on her cheeks felt cold to the touch. Heaven help him, he loved this woman, hated seeing her hurt. And dreaded asking the words at his lips.

"What happened?"

She pulled back, eyed him as her lips quivered, and shook her head. "Sorry I'm such a wreck," she said before blowing out a slow breath. Her shoulders stopped trembling as she repeated the action a second time. "They presented me with a new offer to travel with them and take runway pictures. Monty's going through some rehab program where he's trying to right his past wrongs. They both are, actually. And of course, *I'm* one of the people they wronged. I guess he finally came clean about stealing the images I shot in Milan."

"Wow, that's terrific," Anthony said, but his insides didn't seem to agree. He motioned to the sitting area. *You can handle this,* he assured himself. *Just relax and listen.*

He settled into the center of the couch while Kira plopped onto the leather footrest adjacent to him. She scooted to the edge, slipping her knees between his legs so they were close. Face to face.

"How did he propose to *make things right?*" Anthony asked.

Another slow breath. A few dabs at her face with a bunched-up tissue. "He and Finny wrote up some offer for me to… I guess you'd say go on tour with them. They have a fashion tour coming up, and they want me to shoot the runway pictures."

Anthony nodded. He could handle this. If his body were a planet of its own, ninety percent of it was calm and collected. But a small portion—that other ten percent—was fighting back an underlying tremor. One that could prove destructive if it got out of hand. He wouldn't let it.

"That was nice of them to offer," he said, circling a thumb over her shoulder. "But how could you trust that they wouldn't do the same thing?"

She locked eyes with him and shook her head. "They, it's not like that. But Anthony, it doesn't matter. I shouldn't go."

He grinned. Liking the sound of that. Yet as he ran his hands down the outside of her arms, leaned in to kiss her lips, something she'd said stood out to him: She hadn't said that she didn't *want* to go, only that she *shouldn't.* Those were two very different things.

A hot ache stirred in his chest, and Anthony knew… he knew he couldn't leave it there. The tremor took over another ten percent. "What do you mean by *shouldn't?*" He gulped, willing her *not* to say she'd stay behind for him. He needed her to stay because *she* wanted to.

"I mean," she paused… shook her head. "You've been through so much already. If I went, even if I came right back when I was done, which I totally would, of course, it wouldn't be fair to make you worry that way."

That's all it took. There was a full-on earthquake taking over now. He drew back. "So you'd stay back for *me?*"

She shook her head, just subtly, her brow furrowing. "Of course."

She said it like it's what he'd wanted to hear. Like he hadn't watched his mother walk out of his life after *taking one for the team* and sticking it out as long as she good. "Do me a favor now, and then resent me later. Right?"

Kira's eyes went wide. "No. That's not… it wouldn't be like that at all."

Anthony rose to his feet, resignation kicking in strong. "But that's where you're wrong. Because I've already been through this. I already know how this ends. You stay. You resent me. You end up leaving for good."

"Well then *tell me* what you want me to do?" The look on Kira's pretty face was tortured. Pleading. "*Please...* just tell me."

Anthony walked over to the door, hurt replacing anger as he twisted the knob and tugged it open. "Kira, we both know you want to leave," he said. "So just leave." The words came out calm, but final.

Kira glared at him, shook her head, then bolted out the door.

He didn't walk her to her car. Didn't kiss her goodnight. Or even kiss her goodbye. But mentally, Anthony knew that—for her sake *and* his—telling Kira goodbye was exactly what he had to do.

Kira couldn't remember feeling hurt like this. She replayed

Anthony's words in her head, accompanied by the anger on his face. *Do me a favor now, and resent me later.*

She spun onto her back, stared up at a streak of moonlight peering through her blinds, and smeared the tears on her face. It was no use; a stream of new ones took their place. The heartache of it all just too much to take.

It's what she'd feared most. Anthony taking things the wrong way. Only it'd gone worse than she feared. He hadn't even given her a way out. A new ache tore at her heart, hot and sharp. He'd built her up—said that he trusted her—and then faltered the first chance he got. Maybe she *did* deserve it, by being indecisive and unpredictable in the past. But Anthony really had made her believe that he didn't fear her. So had she betrayed him, or was *he* the betrayer?

It didn't matter. As it was, Kira had shut her sister out, telling her that she'd explain how things went in the morning. Maybe by then she'd be able to explain what had happened. For now, all she could feel was hurt.

CHAPTER 21

"See that spot right there behind you?"

It took Anthony a moment to register what Trent had said. He glanced up to meet his gaze. "What was that?"

"Behind you," Trent said. "There's a gap we need to close. Mind tossing a bag onto it?"

"Oh, yeah. No problem." The sun was barely rising over the pines in the east, lending light on a new day that Anthony wanted no part of. He trudged back to the truck where Bear Schaefer handed over another sandbag.

"There you go, man. Think we're just about there."

"Looks like it," Anthony agreed, lugging the heavy bag to the place in need. He hunched forward, hovered it over the spot, then let it loose. A quick adjustment with the sole of his boot, and the job was done. He strode back toward the fire station, following the building toward the back lot, and leaned his back against the scratchy brick. What had he done? He hadn't even heard Kira out. It was like he'd given up before she even told him about the offer.

Still, he had to admit that—as much as it had hurt to push her away—there'd been an element of relief, too. Something he hated admitting even to himself.

"So things didn't go so well?" Trent asked, joining him behind the building.

"Nope." Not that his demeanor could hide it. "But I'm starting to think that's okay, you know? If I don't have a woman in my life, I don't have to worry about her leaving."

"Ah," Trent said. "I relate to that in a way. You want to know what my biggest setback was with Jessie?"

That caught Anthony's interest; the couple had seemed to be a perfect match from the start. Minus their firework introduction, of course.

"I was in a car accident as a teenager," Trent continued. "My younger brother was in the passenger seat. And I just got reckless, you know? Taking a curve too fast." Trent shook his head, his tone turning quiet. Reverent. "The car rolled over, and he was killed."

"Man," Anthony said. "I didn't know that. I'm sorry..."

Trent nodded. "I told myself that, if I didn't go off and have the life that I took from him, it'd somehow make up for what I did."

Anthony glanced over. "Dedicate your life to helping others instead?"

"Yep. Eventually though, with the help of my loved ones and Jessie, too, I realized I could have both. But it's taken a lot of time for me to get to that point.

"What I'm saying is, you can sit around keeping women out

of your life the way I did, but just like me, you won't be any better off for it. What you'll be... is alone. And I don't think you want that either."

Trent was right. Being alone was the last thing Anthony wanted. "She got an offer to go to Milan and shoot pictures again."

"For how long?"

"I don't know. I didn't let her get that far."

"My old man would always say, *anything worth having comes at a risk,*" Trent said. "And that seems to go right along with what you're facing now. You felt you could trust her, right?"

"Right."

"So what's changed? The fact that she got an offer she'd like to consider? That can't be a crime."

He was right again, but Anthony didn't want to say so.

"You've heard the whole butterfly thing. You're supposed to let them go."

"I've let *enough* women go."

"If she's *yours,*" Trent said, "she'll come back to you. There's only one way to find out."

As he considered that, he recalled the many times he'd had moments of peace and assurance with Kira. Even then, as he heard Trent phrase the question with a big *if* at the start, Anthony already knew how it would go. He felt in his heart that Kira was meant to be his.

He tugged his phone from his pocket to check the time. "You know what?"

"What's that?" Trent asked.

"I think you're right. I better get out to Kira's."

"That's what I'm talking about," Trent said as Anthony started heading toward his truck.

"Hey," Anthony said before climbing in. "Thank you."

Trent grinned. "Any time."

❧

Knocking on a door at this time of morning was just wrong; there was no getting around it. But Anthony couldn't risk losing another minute. Who knew if Kira would have cellular service in places like Milan?

A rustle sounded on the other side of the door. The curtain in the front window moved. "I think it's your boyfriend," crooned a female voice.

The doorknob jiggled before the entire door swung back wide. And there stood a gal Anthony recognized from Kira's pictures. She put her hand out.

"You must be Anthony."

He reached out to shake her hand. "Pleasure. And you must be Marissa."

She grinned. "I am. Come on in. Kira's sulking in the tub."

He lifted a brow. "*Soaking?*"

"No," Marissa said. "*Sulking.* She's upset about how things went last night, but she has yet to tell me why." Her hands went to her hips. "The only thing I know is that it has something to do with you."

Heat flared up in his face. In pictures, it was easy to see the similarities between Kira and her sister. Namely the eyes. But in person, with their personalities as different as they were, they barely resembled one another.

"Well, I'll just go knock on the door, if you don't mind. See if I can't talk with her for a minute."

Marissa did a sidestep, landing squarely in front of him. "You're not going to discourage her, are you?"

He grinned, liking the protective nature he saw in Kira's sister. "No," he said. "Not if it's what she wants." He stepped around her then, moving down the hall to where he tapped on her door. "Kira?"

A loud splash came from the other side of the door. "Anthony?"

"Yes. Can I talk to you?"

A long pause came. "Why?"

"Because I need to apologize. I really messed up last night."

Another splash came, followed by a loud clatter. Something heavy, possibly metal, tumbling to the ground. "Coming," she called.

He heard her mumbling next. Something about the *stupid towel bar*. "I can help you fix that," he assured.

The door opened, revealing a damp-faced Kira in a pink, fluffy robe. She'd made a towel turban for her head, and he'd be danged if it didn't look adorable on her. She folded her arms, leaned in the doorway, and lifted her chin.

"I'm sorry for how I reacted yesterday."

"It's not a decision I asked to make, Anthony."

"I know," he said with a nod.

Her chin quivered. "I would've been happier *not* getting that offer. But I thought it was at least something I could talk to you about. I trusted you."

Trusted? The word was razor sharp.

"We should've been able to discuss that like … two adults

who care about each other, but you made me feel like a criminal or something."

"You're right."

She nodded. Sighed while another beat passed. "Yeah, you didn't even hear me out."

"I know," he admitted. "But I'd like to now. If you'll let me."

Her shoulders dropped, and she did a half-grin. "Really?"

"Very much. You're right. It's something we should discuss... together."

Hmm… She set her gaze on her bare feet while tapping a toe on the tile. "Will you make me some hot chocolate while I tell you about it?" she asked while glancing up.

Anthony piped back a laugh and grinned. "Absolutely."

"Kira," her sister yelled from the front room. "I'm heading to the store now. I'll be right back."

Kira held Anthony's gaze. "Okay," she hollered, a smile curving one side of her lips. "See you in a few."

As soon as the front door closed, Anthony pulled Kira into his arms. "Come here."

Kira returned his embrace, the damp towel pressing against his face as she sighed.

He pulled back, rested his hands on her cheeks, and held her gaze. "I really am sorry," he said.

Kira nodded, snatched his arm and led him into the kitchen. There, Anthony took over. He guided her to a barstool before snatching the kettle and filling it with fresh water. Once it was heating over the gas flames of her stove, Anthony pulled two mugs from the cupboard. His homemade blend of hot cocoa rested in the copper canister on the baker's rack. Kira retrieved it for him before he could ask. "Now," he said. "Tell me everything."

They sipped on mugs filled with hot cocoa, a layer of whipped cream bobbing along the top, as Kira did just that. There were no interruptions from Anthony this time. No accusations either. He simply listened to the details of the offer before her.

"Anyway," Kira said, tipping her mug to the side and scraping her spoon along the edge. "I feel a million times better now that I've been able to get that off my chest. I honestly… hate the idea of leaving, so it's easy to say no." She popped a heap of cream into her mouth.

Anthony was surprised to find that Trent's words really had started to sink in. Kind of like the moment he'd sat next to Kira by the fireplace and told her—in all honesty—that he wasn't afraid of the choices she might make. He cleared his throat. "I'm not sure that you *need* to say no, Kira."

She yanked the spoon from her mouth. Her face fell flat. "*What?*" The word sounded angry.

"I'm looking at this offer," he said, fanning the pages of the documents she'd spread over the counter. "I have a lawyer who can look over it this morning. He'll make sure the offer's legit, of course, but if it is… this would be a great opportunity for you."

"I don't get it. *You* think I should go too?"

Anthony could hardly believe it himself. He was really putting his money where his mouth was, as the saying went. But he trusted her. Trusted that *here* is where she wanted to stay. And she could. *After* she tied up some loose ends. "I know that you can take this opportunity," he said. "And that it's not going to change your mind about what you want to do." At least, he thought he knew. Hoped. "This is a chance for you to get *redemption*. You deserve that. *Recognition*. You deserve that too. Not to mention a pretty nice paycheck. I fully support you. Go spend forty-five awesome days traveling the world and snapping pictures." He reached his arms across the counter, cupped her hands in his. "And then come back to me. To the life you've found here. The one that makes you happy. I'll be waiting."

CHAPTER 22

Kira stared blankly at the goings-on in the airport and tuned in to the warmth of Anthony's hand on her back. She would miss that for the next month and a half. "I can't believe I'm really going."

Anthony nodded. "You're going to do great."

"Right." Marissa had boarded her plane over an hour ago, which gave Anthony and Kira a little more time to say goodbye to one another. She was grateful for everything he'd had done for her in the last few hours. He'd set up an emergency meeting with his attorney, Jed, and made sure everything Finny offered was put in writing, all the way down to the public apology in at least six different media sources. He'd stood upright and tall in the face of her ex, his confidence never wavering. He'd even taken the initiative to shake Monty's hand, thank him and Finny for making things right, and wish them a safe trip.

Anthony Marino had said the words once—told Kira that he

believed in her. But now he was putting that into action. Strong-as-titanium action. She couldn't remember feeling so loved.

"Just a few more minutes ..." He pressed a kiss to her head. "I'm going to miss you, Kira."

She nodded. "I'm going to miss you too."

"But I can't wait to hear about everything." He came to a stand, looped her bags around his shoulder, and took her hand. "C'mon," he said. "We better get you on that plane."

Kira did a mental check of her list after boarding the jet. She'd called everyone in her scheduling book for the next forty-five days and either rescheduled or referred them to one of the backups Gramps had on his list. A few he trusted that were located in Duckdale Hollow. The ones she hadn't been able to get a hold of, she'd passed on to her new tenant, Alexia. The talented artist had agreed to be her secretary while she was away. In exchange, Kira would waive her rent for the next two months.

Thank heavens she'd finished up with the senior pictures. She would have felt horrible for missing one of those, since they'd had their hearts set on the whole personalized graffiti thing.

Luckily, Finny Shea, and Python (she'd have to get used to calling him that) had taken the front corner of the jet and allowed Kira to occupy the opposite corner in back. Forty-five days. Runways, hectic schedules, and time demands. Anthony had told Kira not to wish her time away, said that she needed to enjoy the experience as best she could. She'd try. But already Kira was looking forward to the day it'd all be over. Her name would be cleared, and then she'd be back with Anthony where she belonged.

CHAPTER 23

Anthony sank under the covers and brought the phone closer to his ear. "So you actually shot Abigail Rylie?"

Kira chuckled from the other end. "In the flesh. But be careful how you say that. Don't want it to sound like the kind with a handgun."

He grinned, sank his head deeper into his pillow. "True."

"Did you kick some tail in poker tonight?" she asked.

"Kicked trash and took names, baby."

"That's my man!"

Anthony loved when he could hear the smile in her voice. "Don't you forget it."

"Never."

It remained quiet as he basked in the moment. Content. They'd done it. Kira had almost fulfilled her contract, and Anthony had stayed behind, run the diner, and not gone insane.

"Two more days," she purred.

The words were ear candy, especially to the tune of that sultry voice. "I know."

"I can't wait."

"Me neither." She sighed. "Oh man, it's four-thirty. You're going to have to get into the diner soon."

"I know," he said with a groan. "When you get back, I don't want to live another day without you." He rubbed a hand over his face, realizing that sounded a whole lot like a proposal.

"Then don't," Kira said.

More silence. A peace-filled space that allowed Anthony's mind to soar to the sky.

"Good night," she said.

He nodded, cleared his throat. "Good night."

CHAPTER 24

Kira took a sip from her drink and rested her head back on the beach chair. Barcelona was beautiful. The weather was perfect for soaking in a little sun while unwinding from their hectic schedule. Kira had to take advantage of the hotel's massive pool and cabana at least one day before leaving.

Finny and Python had been more than civil throughout the tour; it was evident that they were truly repentant after all.

"Excuse me," a voice came from behind. A woman, the one who'd brought Kira her drink, stood there. A small apron was wrapped around her waist. "I couldn't help but overhear your conversation. Hope you don't mind. But you're the one traveling with Finny Shea and her fashion team, right? You're their new photographer?"

"Yeah," Kira said with a nod.

"And you left home to come out here with them, and now you're headed back?"

She gave her another nod. "Yes."

The woman didn't have an accent like many on the island did. But her skin held a nice olive complexion. Her hair was smooth and black, and her eyes were the deepest brown. Kind eyes, with a beautiful smile to match.

"You know, I just want to tell you that … that you're very lucky to be returning home as you are. A lot of people, they chase dream after dream until they don't even remember who they are anymore."

Kira sighed. "I feared I might do that myself at first, but I fell in love with a man who trusts me. He knew I'd come back. And it gave me the confidence I needed to believe in myself."

The woman nodded absently. "This might seem silly, but do you mind if I confide in you?"

A band of warmth tightened around her heart as she took in the tears welling in the woman's eyes. "Please," she said. "I've got all day. Have a seat if you'd like." She motioned to the chair beside her.

The woman tipped her head to eye the clock in the cabana. "Okay," she said. "I *don't* have all day, but I've got a fifteen-minute break. Close enough."

Kira sat up, lifted her hat off the glass side table, and rested it on her head. *There.* Now she wouldn't have to squint.

"Years ago, I left a place and a man that I loved, too. I had every intention to return. I thought if I sowed some wild oats, I'd be a better person for it." She wiped her face, rubbed her lips together before continuing. "The first place I went just … it wasn't what I hoped it would be. So I tried something else. And then something else. And before I knew it, seven years had gone by. Seven whole years. It was like I'd lost track along the way. I was ready to go back at that point, but I couldn't get myself to do it. I told myself that ... well, that they probably hated me by then. For leaving them like I did. They'd never take me back. Even if my husband hadn't remarried, which I figure after seven years he probably had, but even if he hadn't, he wouldn't want me. Neither of them would."

Kira tipped her head. "I'm sorry, *neither of them?* So it was more than just your husband?"

"Maria," a voice called from deep inside the cabana. "Break's over."

The woman gave him a nod. "Coming." She turned back to Kira. "Yes, it was more." Her face scrunched up in a word she could only describe as agony. Like the face Kira probably made when she contemplated leaving Anthony behind. "I left behind a child too. I hate myself for it. But I guess this is just ... who I am. I can't change it now."

She hurried to her feet then, wrapping the apron snuggly around her waist once more, and patted Kira on the knee. "You are a very blessed woman. I want you to know that."

"Thanks," Kira said through a teary grin. "I appreciate that."

She leaned back in her chair, covered her face with the hat, and let the exchange run through her mind once more. The woman's story triggered something inside her. Something just barely out of reach.

Kira couldn't guess why, but her mind shifted back to the moment she and Anthony were at the bowling alley. When he'd described his tattoo. *"Three M's,"* he'd said. *"For my mother, Maria."*

Goose bumps rushed over her arms as Kira climbed off the chair, sending her hat to the hot cement in the process. "Hey,

Maria?" she hollered before she'd even placed her. Eyes squinted against the bright sun as Kira peered deep into the cabana.

"Yes?" Her voice came from someplace near the pool.

Kira spun around. "You said you left a man and a child. Was it a daughter or a son?"

The woman tilted her head. Smiled softly. "A son. My Anthony, named after his father."

CHAPTER 25

Anthony had spent a whole lot of his life in the *what-if* phase. Starting at a young age. What if Mom never comes back? He'd carried that concern with him ever since.

What if Ruth leaves? Which she had. What if Elsie leaves? Well, that happened too. It seemed as if he spent his life chasing people away with doubt and fear.

His mind drifted back to a quote Pops had framed and placed on his dresser. 1 John 4:18. "*Perfect love casts out fear.*"

Anthony hadn't understood it back then. Yet somewhere between losing his dad, meeting Kira, and falling deeply in love with her, he'd learned to give up that fear. Not that his love for her would ever be perfect or his trust, for that matter. But he'd grown in both aspects. Just in time to love Kira the way she needed to be loved. He hadn't done it alone. Besides the good Lord, Anthony figured that Pops and Angelo had something to do with it. After all, how else could he explain the chain of events that had unfolded over the last few months?

A deeper relationship with Kira. The job offer that came along—the one that led Kira to the woman she met in Barcelona at the tail end of her trip just two days ago. Turned out Finny and Python were sold on the goal of making amends, and were thrilled to assist his mother's effort to do that very thing.

Anthony couldn't get his leg to stop bouncing. Seated in the same place he and Kira sat a month-and-a-half ago, the exact bench, even, he waited to see the two most important women in his life. One who was destined to be a daily part of his future—she'd assured him of that before leaving, and every day since. The other woman, whom he hadn't seen in twenty years … well, only time would tell what she planned to do. He hoped his mother would stick around and be a part of their lives, but he wouldn't press her on it. Kira had chosen Cobble Creek. She'd chosen him. And as far as he was concerned, the rest was gravy.

He shifted his gaze back to the screen, noticing that the flight had landed. He stood and paced behind the bench, his eyes flicking from the scuff-marked floor to the arrival gate then back again. A crowd of people filtered through. A large family with everything from teenagers to babies. An older couple with sunburns and visors. Probably been somewhere tropical.

"Hey there, handsome," came that sultry voice he loved.

Anthony stopped walking, yanked his gaze off the moving crowd, and glanced behind him. "How did you …"

"I snuck under the dividers." Kira rushed in and threw her arms around him. "Your mom went to the ladies' room to freshen up."

A mixture of emotions flowed through him. In mere

moments, he'd see his mother for the first time in twenty years. But first … he lifted Kira off the ground and spun her in place. *Home at last.* Warm and loving and everything he wanted in a woman. Kira had come back to him, just as he'd known she would. He breathed in her sweet strawberry scent and sighed. "I missed you so much."

Kira pulled back and grinned. "I missed you too." Suddenly she was kissing his face. Cheeks, forehead, the tip of his nose. Covering every inch in short, hurried kisses. "Mwah. Mwah. Mwah. And …" She brought her lips to his mouth and pressed a kiss there too. "Mwah! Hi," she breathed against his lips.

"Hi," he rasped.

"This feels so good," Kira said, nuzzling into his neck. "I missed your face and your voice and your smell."

Anthony tipped his head back. "My smell?"

"Yes," Kira crooned in that sultry voice that drove him mad. She lowered her chin and looked at him through fluttering lashes. "I'm so happy to be back in Cobble Creek."

Kira slipped her palms down Anthony's arm and sandwiched his hand between hers. "She'll be coming out that doorway any minute. Can you believe it?" She nodded toward a nearby lavatory, the wide walkway adjacent to the men's room.

The noise and chaos might have marched on, but Anthony tuned it all out. Channeling the few memories he had of the woman. Loving memories. Her lovely face as she slid a root beer float across the bar, the foamy layer tilting like sea foam on an ocean tide. *"It's all yours, Tony boy."*

And then there was the memory of being at the pond with her. She'd spread out a blanket so the two could watch ducks bathe in the water. The memory centered around one particular moment when she tossed her arms over her head and declared, "Watch out, world, here I come!" And then she plopped back onto the blanket, grinning wide. "Come on, Tony boy. Try it." In his memory, he'd done just that. Tossed his arms up, hollered those same words, and then flattened onto his back, where the two giggled. He couldn't remember what came next. But he used to imagine that she reached out to test all those ticklish spots Dad used to poke at to make him laugh whether he felt like it or not.

Through the vision of his musings, a woman striding from the indicated doorway came into clear focus. Black hair. Oval-shaped face. And a lifetime of mystery behind her eyes. *Her.* It was unmistakably *her.* The face from those memories.

"Oh, my Tony boy," she whispered as she neared. With trembling hands, she reached out to him, patted his face as tears rolled down her cheeks. "Do you mind … I mean, is it okay if I hug you?"

He nodded, working to hold back emotions of his own.

At once her arms were wrapped solidly around him. "I'm so sorry," she cried. "I'm so sorry for leaving you." She held on to him as she wept a moment more, then seemed to remember herself. When she pulled away, she patted his arm before glancing over at Kira.

"How about we grab our luggage and get to the car," Kira suggested. "We can catch up some more there."

They did that very thing, the conversation flowing comfortably between Kira and his mother. Simple things. A joke about the contrast between the private jet that had taken them from Barcelona to LA, and the commercial flight they'd taken to come to Wyoming. It struck him just how *human* his mother really was. Crazy.

In the truck, she started up where she'd left off. Seated in the far passenger seat while Kira sat buckled in the center, Maria spoke of her regret.

"I'm sorry I wasn't here when your father died. You don't know what it did to me when Kira told me he'd passed." She wiped tears from her face as she said it, her words choked out by sobs. She explained that for the first few years, she was caught up in herself. But for the last thirteen-plus years, she thought about coming back every day, yet feared it was too late. That he and his dad would hate her.

Anthony stopped her there. "We never could've hated you." It might have come out low and mumbled, but he'd meant it.

His mother had offered words that would take years for Anthony to digest. But in the moment, among all the emotions and tears, one word stood out like it'd been wrapped in construction orange: *fear.* He hadn't been the only one held back by it over the years.

Yesterday, while telling the guys about Kira's discovery, Benny asked if Anthony was mad at his mother. The answer hadn't been simple. After struggling over the question for a bit, Anthony finally said that he wasn't sure.

But now, with the woman he loved by his side, expelling *awkward tension* like there'd never been such thing, a strong spirit of forgiveness took over. When they had more time to talk, he'd make sure Maria understood that very important truth. He wasn't interested in holding grudges and dwelling on the past. Instead, Anthony was focused on his future.

CHAPTER 26

Kira zoomed in on a brightly colored Easter egg as Harper led a cluster of toddlers toward a hidden egg. Holding tight to one hand was Phillip, Maddie and Bear's nephew. Dressed in a white shirt and bowtie, a chocolate smear over his lip, he was the perfect match for the toddler gripping on to Harper's right hand: Benny & Darcie's little girl. Sure, the dainty one had on a frilly dress with lace gloves and a matching hat to go with it, but that little lady wasn't messing around. Her small face scrunched as they neared, her eyes fixed on whatever part of the egg she could see.

Kira twisted the lens, bringing the tiny blonde into focus, and snapped a few shots. She zoomed out enough to capture a colorful egg in soft focus at the forefront, the small treasure tucked into a gnarled bend of a bark-covered tree. She captured more shots as the child rested the egg in her grass-heaped basket, only to have it tumble right out and onto the ground. Little Phillip came to the rescue, though, swooping it up with messy fingers and pressing it back into her basket where it belonged.

Marissa, who'd attempted to watch from the sidelines, had been dragged into the action by a curly-haired Callie, a little gal related to a woman who helped run the B&B. Kira's mom and dad had come into town with her sister this time, which made the holiday even more special. Her parents had surprised her by helping the bunch color eggs at Tony's Diner the day before. They also agreed to meet with the volunteers early that morning to hide them all at Lakeview Park. Of course, not all of them were actual eggs. Many were plastic eggs stuffed with goodies and stickers, press-on tattoos of baby chicks and fluffy bunnies. That was part of the magic of Cobble Creek: empty nesters, single adults, newly marrieds, or someplace in between, there was a place for everyone.

It took Kira a moment, among the excitement, to locate Anthony, but at last she did. Perhaps it was due to the growing number of kids surrounding him. Or rather, the giant bunny Anthony was guiding through the park. Seth, bless him, had volunteered to be Cobble Creek's Easter Bunny. Trouble was, the limited visibility caused him to stumble. A lot. Anthony caught her attention across the way and reached up to give her a wave. "Hello over there."

"How's it going?" she asked. He held her gaze, the heat it always brought zooming through her chest.

"Oh no!" one kid hollered.

"The Easter Bunny's clumsy," another called out.

Kira glanced down to see Seth stumbling over a diaper bag. She could hardly hold back a laugh.

Anthony shot into action. "The Easter Bunny isn't seeing

very well today. I think he forgot to eat his carrots."

"The Easter Bunny's a girl," little Callie hollered.

Anthony shot Kira a questioning glance.

"Okay," Kira said with a laugh. Good thing Seth was such a good sport. "Lead *her* to the pond, will you, Anthony? It's time for pictures."

Kira's parents waited on a bench beside Maria, who busily tucked tulips into a watering can she'd found at Frank & Signs. The woman had an artistic eye, and she wasn't afraid to use it. In the eight-plus months she'd been there, Anthony's mom had become Kira's assistant. She was talented, hardworking, and kind. And most of all, she seemed to savor each day like a precious gift. Kira was challenging herself to do the same.

"Hop, hop, hop," Kira heard as she headed toward the water's edge. She stopped, spun to see what the hollering was about, and grinned wide at the sight. What had once been clusters of kids making their way to the pond was now a line of bunny impersonators, happily hopping as they followed the leaders—Anthony and Seth, that is. Tiny giggles drifted from the trail. Several parents joined in on the action, and Kira paused to shoot a few pictures of the sight. Judy, the gal who ran the police station, would probably pin a few on the community board at the rec center.

Once they made their way to the prepared spot for the photo shoot, Kira guided Seth to the special Easter Bunny chair. The kids lined up, and Kira got straight to business. Seth was great with the kids. Anthony was, too, distracting the little ones who'd been scared to tears at the sight of the giant bunny. It was a side of him she hadn't seen a whole lot. Harper helped out, too, pulling a special egg from the Easter Bunny's basket and handing it to each child before they shuffled back to the crowd gathered by a nearby tree. Once they were through, Harper pulled a gold-colored egg from the basket. It was smaller than the others, and stood out next to the pastel ones she'd handed out.

"Mind if I shoot a few candid photos of the group, since we're done with the posed ones?" Maria asked.

"Not at all." Kira shrugged out of the camera strap and handed it over, glad Maria was interested in learning to shoot. It would help out a whole lot if Kira had an assistant who could take photos on her own if needed.

"Anthony," Harper called out. "It looks like this egg is for you."

"It *does*?" Anthony asked with a lifted brow. "Are you sure?"

Harper handed it over to Seth, who held it with white, furry paws. "Oh yeah, this one's his, all right."

Anthony laughed. "That doesn't make any sense, but … okay." He rolled his eyes and leaned into Kira. "Seth's probably pulling some sort of prank. May as well play along."

Kira watched as he headed over.

"What's going on?" Maria asked.

"He said something about the egg being for him," Kira's dad mumbled in reply. Kira hadn't even realized her parents had broken away from the shaded area to join her.

"The Easter Bunny has a special egg for Anthony," Phillip hollered.

By the time Anthony had the small egg in his hands, the crowd had gathered in. A hush fell over the group as he held it up, inspecting it with tight lips and narrowed eyes.

"What is it?" Callie asked.

"I'm not sure," he mumbled. "But I think Kira might."

Kira tilted her head. "Huh?"

"Come here," he said, motioning her to join him at the center of the group.

"Go on," Marissa urged with a nudge.

Kira broke away from the spectators and walked along the small, pebbled trail leading to Anthony. Green grass swayed at either side as a breeze blew in. A breeze that lent her a dose of anticipation. She tried to dissect the odd situation, feeling as if she were missing something. But it wasn't until Anthony lowered himself onto one knee that she realized what that something might be.

He palmed the small egg before prying it back, the open face in her direction.

Kira's heartbeat kicked up, thumping like a rabbit's as she peeked inside. There, tucked in a black velvet fold, shone a gorgeous diamond ring. Several audible gasps broke out over the crowd, but none were as loud as Kira's. "Anthony?" His name practically fell off her lips.

His brown eyes were set on her, that warm smile of his causing the bunny thumps to drop to her tummy. He glanced toward the pond, where the cattails bounced and swayed beside the glistening water.

"When I was a little boy, a girl from out of town came and dragged me to this very pond. She was a lot of fun, a little mischievous, and one of the cutest girls I'd ever seen. And now that she's grown ..." He cleared his throat as moisture welled up in his eyes. "I can say that she's brilliant and fascinating, and of course, the most beautiful woman I've ever seen. And if she'll let me, I'd love to spend the rest of my life with her."

Kira's chest swelled, her body barely able to contain the bliss that pulsed through her.

"My Kira Kira, will you marry me?"

It was in that moment that Kira realized everyone had stepped in closer. A few whispers sounded among the kids.

"What's she gonna say?"

"I hope she says yes."

Kira grinned. "Yes! Of *course* I'll marry you!" She barely gave Anthony a chance to stand before she pulled him in for a kiss.

Whistles, claps, and cheers rose in celebration as they spun in place.

"Put the ring on her," Seth hollered.

Anthony nodded. "Oh, yeah." All eyes moved back to the egg-shaped case as Anthony pinned the shimmering ring between his finger and thumb. He closed the case before sliding the ring onto her finger with a jittery hand. Turned out she wasn't the only one shaking. More cheers sounded as Kira held up her hand.

"Right here," Maria hollered, camera aimed and ready. Which explained why she'd asked for the camera when she had. Kira was grateful Anthony's sweet mom was there to not only witness the special moment, but to capture it, too.

Anthony nuzzled into her, running the tip of his nose along her cheek. "I can't wait for you to be my wife," he crooned.

"I mean, I can't wait either!" And as she caught sight of the cattails swaying in the distance, Kira had the distinct impression that—though Gramps couldn't be there to celebrate with them—he'd helped send Maria to take his place. What an unexpected gift it was. Mysterious ways indeed, but Kira wouldn't change it for the world.

EPILOGUE

Most women spoke of their dream wedding. Marissa had been speaking of hers since she turned eight years old, according to Mom, anyway. But Kira was different. She'd always hoped to marry the man of her dreams one day, but the wedding part never mattered much to her. Luckily, her sister had been there to "make magic happen," if she said so herself. And the truth was, she *had.*

Perhaps Marissa had missed *her* true calling. Goodbye middle school teaching day in and day out—hello wedding planner.

"Let me see you," Connie said. "Blot your lips right here." She shoved a folded paper towel between Kira's parted lips, and Kira obeyed. Connie and Marlene, owners of CC's Salon, had come to the Country Quilt B&B over an hour ago and been working wonders on her since.

"Look in the mirror and make sure we didn't go overboard," Connie said. "Your sister was adamant about that."

Kira blew out a slow breath and spun to look in the mirror. Before her eyes landed on her own reflection, she spotted Marissa and her mom in the background, their focus set on her. She grinned, fighting back tears as she noticed the moisture in their eyes.

"No crying," Marlene said. "It'll mess your face up."

But Kira could hardly help it. It had taken a long time to develop the relationship she had with the women in the mirror, and now that she had, it enhanced every beautiful thing about the special day.

"You look stunning," her mom said with a sniff.

"Perfect," Marissa agreed. "I knew she should have part of her hair down in back with the twist like that," she added under her breath. It was like watching Gramps admire his own masterpiece.

At last she flicked her gaze to her own reflection, liking the woman she saw looking back at her. A woman who'd learned to trust herself.

"Well?" Connie urged.

"It's good," she said, glad they hadn't gone overboard on the makeup. "Perfect."

The group rushed in with oohs and aahs, patting at her carefully to avoid messing up her hair or her dress or her perfectly rouged cheeks.

"Tony's gonna flip out," Maria said.

Kira hadn't even seen her come back in. Earlier, Maria had stepped in with the camera, snapping shots of Marissa and her mother helping her get ready. But she'd taken off to go see how things were going in the groom's room.

Kira caught Maria's gaze as the crowd of women cleared. "Is

he ready?" Thoughts of Anthony in a tux made her heart sprout wings or feet or whatever it was that made it jump wildly in her chest.

"Oh, he's ready, all right. He says he's been waiting for this moment his whole life."

"Awww ..." the women cooed in chorus.

"And he looks unbelievably handsome," his mother added with a wink.

"Well, let's get her out there," Marissa said. She walked over to the doorway of the bride's room and spoke with Jessie, the owner of the B&B, who'd been helping with the arrangements. Kira would've never thought to do a twilight ceremony outdoors, but Marissa and Jessie were convinced that the back patio at the Country Quilt Inn would offer the perfect twilight setting.

The music began, its gentle sound drifting through the windows where Kira awaited her cue. At last, Jessie popped her head through the doorway. "Okay," she whispered, "your dad's ready for you."

Kira stood, took a few steps toward the open doorway, and grinned as her father came into view. He looked a lot like Gramps in the moment, with his thick, dark hair turning silver along his hairline.

"Kira ..." He smeared the back of his fist beneath each reddened eye. "You look beautiful."

"Thanks, Dad. You look great too." He wasn't a man of many words, but as he took her arm in his, pressing his palm over the back of her hand, she knew he was proud of her. Of the woman she'd become.

She gripped fistfuls of her dress as they made their way out the back exit, an outdoor stairwell that led to the waiting guests. Marissa and Jessie had been right about the setting. *So* right. It stole Kira's breath as she took it all in. A cranberry sunset shimmered off the distant pond while industrial-looking light bulbs hung generously throughout the seating area, each light catching hints of the colorful sunset. Tall vases holding white flowers were spread amply throughout the deck. Beside each vase, a collection of photo frames held pictures of the happy couple, each illuminated by a cluster of twinkle lights. *Beautiful!*

Prior to this moment, Kira hadn't been able to imagine what it might look like, with things set up the way her sister and Jessie explained. And now she knew why—it was beyond anything her mind could have.

She took in the faces of so many people she knew and loved. New friends she'd made in Cobble Creek. Family. Even her great-aunts in their white hats and lace gloves blotted at tears as Dad escorted her down the aisle. But just ahead … tall and handsome, beside Pastor John, stood Anthony Marino. At a distance, it reminded her of shooting runway photos. The models working to master that look of head-to-toe perfection. Anthony outdid them all.

As she stepped closer, following the trail of white and pink rose petals scattered along the wood planked deck, their eyes met. He held her gaze, a stunned expression on his face, then he snapped his mouth shut and gulped.

Kira grinned, glanced down, and blew out a slow-paced breath. *That's the man I'll be married to for the rest of my life …* She could hardly believe it.

Things moved quickly from that point on. Thank heavens

Darcy and Benny volunteered to record the ceremony. As much as Kira tried memorizing every precious word, look, and touch exchanged during their vows, she couldn't possibly remember it all.

"Go on and kiss your bride," Pastor John said once the rings were in place.

Anthony reached out and cradled Kira's face. "My bride," he murmured, a breath before his mouth took hers.

The men cheered, the ladies oohed and aahed once more, and Kira nearly lost her balance as she sank into a moment she wanted a whole lot more of. In his vows, Anthony promised to cherish her forever. And Kira had done the same. But even forever had to be taken one day at a time. And from this moment on, Kira planned to cherish each day she had with the man she loved.

SAMPLE CHAPTER FROM REESE'S COWBOY KISS

Thanks for reading The Determined Bride. Enjoy more small town romance with this sample chapter from Reese's Cowboy Kiss, Book One of the Sweet Montana Bride Series.

Reese's Cowboy Kiss

Chapter One

Reese glanced over the large crowd of dancing bodies as she caught her breath. It hadn't been easy to keep up with the fast-paced line dance in a gown and high heels, but she'd be lying if she said it hadn't been fun. Still, it was almost time to pass off her crown to this year's winner, and she needed to freshen up.

With a shallow sigh, she searched the crowd once more, glad when she failed to see the man with the unyielding gaze. The gawking stranger had set her on edge since she'd arrived. Perhaps he'd gone home, she decided, feeling hopeful at the mere thought.

The rowdy song came to an end while she moved along the outskirts of the dance floor. A warm Texas breeze wafted over her skin just as the band started a new tune – a slow and easy number. The kind that had her picturing warm days at the lake. Or romantic strolls on a moonlit night. She smiled as a young couple among the group caught her attention. Their intimate contact seeming to reach into that longing place in her heart. Reese's glance shifted to the man's hand, clenched around the woman's waist as he kissed her, passion oozing from his every move. Never had she been kissed in such a manner. Or even known a man she wished would kiss her that way.

"Some folks just don't know when to get a room," a familiar voice spoke.

Reese spun around to see her younger brother, CJ, standing close by. Her face flushed with heat as her gaze fell back to the couple. "Yeah," she agreed with a sigh. "I guess you're right."

"Why ain't you dancin' with nobody?" CJ asked. "Too big of a snob?"

She slapped his arm. "You know I'd never turn anyone down. I'm just looking for Mama, is all. She's got my makeup bag."

"Well, wish I could help ya, but I'm off to find a pretty little thing to dance with." He flashed her a mischievous grin, rolling his shoulders back.

"You enjoy yourself," she said. "And don't you go makin' out on the dance floor."

Her brother cocked one eyebrow, gave her a wink, and then disappeared into the crowd. Reese's gaze wandered to the auction tables along the stage. And there was her mom, frantically scribbling on a tattered notepad.

The lights on the stage were bright against the night, causing Reese to squint as she moved. She'd made it only part-way up the steps when a wiry hand clamped around her wrist.

"Would you like to dance?"

Reese spun around, knowing who'd asked before even seeing the man. She forced a polite smile as her fears were confirmed. It was him – the man who'd burned holes straight through her body with his steely glare alone. He was fairly thin, but his features were soft and round; from the outline of his clean-shaven jaw, to his small nose and bulbous cheeks. He blinked a few times, his bright green eyes watering from the blaring stage lights.

"I'd love to," she lied, guessing the makeup would have to wait. Her peace of mind would be put on hold too, but it was just one dance. She could get through it.

His clammy fingers skidded down her wrist to where he took hold of her hand, pulling her deep into the crowd before settling on a spot. Reese grimaced, suddenly feeling like a giant. With the help of her three-inch heels, she was half-a-head taller than the guy.

He glanced up at her, the intensity she'd seen in his eyes replaced by something entirely different. Reese tilted her head; she'd made a habit of looking for the inner light in folks – that unique spark that made each person shine. She could usually sense it quickly enough. A humble kindness or confident gleam. A determined spirit or forgiving heart. Surely this guy was no exception.

Or was he? She furrowed her brows as she looked at him further, unable to get past the odd shifting of his eyes. The strange way he evaded her gaze.

He was simply shy, Reese decided, as he stepped closer and wrapped his arms around her back. She rested her hands on his shoulders in return, unnerved by his tense and rigid form. Her skin objected to him too. The very feel of him against her was all wrong.

There was an obvious rhythm to the slow song playing, but the guy barely lifted a foot. Reese had danced with several men that evening. Everything from true Texas gentlemen to cocky, bull riding brutes. But none of them had made her feel the way this guy did. On edge. Almost … afraid. She pulled in a deep breath, counting down the seconds, dying for the song to end. She felt guilty for being so turned off by the man; he was obviously nervous. Most likely he'd simply been working up the nerve to ask her to dance as he'd stared throughout the evening. Why couldn't she be endeared to him instead?

The answer stood in the energy surrounding him; it felt off. Eager. Intense. And as much as she wanted to make polite conversation to ease the discomfort of it all, she couldn't think of a word to say. He'd just have to be the one to speak up first.

Yet as the band played on, the odd stranger never uttered a word. And as ugly as it felt, staying silent as they danced, Reese did just that.

At last the music began to fade as a deep voice blared from the stage – Corbin Carmichael, the host of the annual event. "One last song, folks," he announced, "and then our Pearland Rose and our new title holder will take the stage for the passing of the crown." Hoots, hollers, and cat calls sounded from the crowd. "Now let's hear one more round of applause for our rip roaring band for the night, the Texan Blasters. I wanna see all y'all on the dance floor for this one. Time to get those boots a stompin'!"

Reese cleared her throat and backed away from the awkward man, causing him to drop his arms at last. "Thanks for the dance," she said, turning away from him. She was anxious to be free from the man, to find her mom, and to get freshened up before passing on her crown.

It was that tight and sudden grip around her wrist that stopped her short, a repeat of what he'd done the first time. His palm felt cool and wet. "Guess it's time to finally give up your title," the young man said. "I'm really going to miss seeing you in that crown."

Reese's gaze had been set on the grip he had on her. She glanced over to the bodies stepping to the line dance before looking into the man's face. Beads of sweat coated his forehead and upper lip. The surface of his cheeks looked red and swollen. "I hardly ever wore the thing," she said.

"You wore it to all your public appearances." His fingers loosened the slightest bit. The corner of his lip twitched.

Reese nodded, his intrusive gaze causing her to shift; the striking green of his eyes becoming oddly familiar. "Do I know you from somewhere?" she asked.

"High school," he explained. "I'm Donald Turnsbro. We were in Mr. Li's biology class together."

"That's right," she said. Only she couldn't actually place him. It'd been five years since high school after all. The crowd started to move in on them, forcing their bodies close once more. "Well, thanks again for the dance," Reese said. "I better go freshen up." She darted toward the stage, barely dodging a collision with the dancers on the floor. She folded her arms over her chest as she sped up the stairs, recalling the way he'd reached for her wrist; the recollection making her shiver.

She spotted her mom next to the auction table, arranging paper slips next to each item sold. "Mama?"

A large smile spread over her face as she spun around. "Hi, darlin'. You're going to be up in just a bit."

Reese remained motionless as she adjusted the hair around her crown. "Is it a mess?" she asked.

"Nah, I've seen worse. But here, you'll be wanting this." She spun around and began scrounging under the picnic table at the edge of the stage, the curtain barely covering the mess of tote bags, Tupperware, and boxes. "Here." She handed over her makeup bag. "Doesn't look like there's a line to the ladies room. Why don't you sneak on in there."

A deep sigh made its way through Reese's chest as she tucked the small bag under her arm. "Thank you."

"What's a matter, baby? Sad about giving up your crown?"

Reese shrugged, looking over the crowd for the strange man. "Maybe a little."

Her mom placed her hands on Reese's cheeks, waited until her gaze settled back on her. "Well there's a bright side to it, ya know? Close your eyes and take a whiff."

Reese looked back at her warily.

"Trust me, baby. Just do it."

While releasing another sigh, Reese closed her eyes. Her mom's hands moved to Reese's upper arms. "Now," she said, "inhale a nice, deep breath."

Reese inhaled until her chest rose.

"What do you smell?" she asked her.

"I don't know."

A chuckle escaped her mom's lips. "Boy, you *have* been dieting for a while. Haven't ya? Try again."

Reese focused as she breathed in, noting the incredible aroma, thick on the evening air. Rich and smoky, tangy and sweet. "Barbeque," she said. "Smells just like Grandma Dee's."

"That's right. And you don't have to worry about fitting into these gowns or keeping trim for any special events. Soon as you hand over that crown, let the new girl count calories and you go get some *real* food."

Reese gasped. "Mama," she said with a chuckle. "I can't believe my ears."

"What? I ain't suggesting you let yourself go completely. But you need to take advantage of the perks of *not* being Miss Pearland's Rose."

Reese smiled. "Yeah, maybe you're right." Her mouth watered at the thought.

"That-a girl. Now skedaddle on outta here and go freshen up." Her mom had managed to distract her from the disturbing encounter with the strange man; Reese was grateful for it. She always did know how to make things right.

Feeling a bit more at ease, Reese sped toward the restrooms behind the stage. She gripped hold of the thick, black curtain along the sidewall, knowing the bathroom doors were entirely hidden by the thing, and spotted a man among the hefty cloth.

Her heart jumped.

She tilted her head, anxious to get a better look at his face, when he disappeared into the fabric folds. With renewed force, Reese shoved the curtain aside once more, wondering if her mind was playing tricks on her. She might not have gotten a solid look at him, but the man she'd seen looked just like Donald Turnsbro; she was sure of it.

Her hands trembled slightly as she tugged the curtain back one last time, knowing she was in the right place. And there it was, the sign she'd been looking for, the letters carved right into the bathroom door: *Senoritas.*

Anxious thumps pressed their way through her chest as she pried open the heavy oak door, desperate to get into the quiet space and grip hold of her rampant thoughts.

The music died down as the door closed behind her, the soft glow of light a welcoming change. She skipped the mirror altogether and sped straight for the only stall. Reese had the door partway closed before she noticed a young woman standing at the sink. She tilted her head to catch eye contact with her through the mirror. Blonde hair, a sash over her shoulder, and a dress that matched the color of Reese's gown.

"Howdy," Reese offered with a shaky voice.

The girl blinked her lashes through a wand of mascara before glancing at her. "Can't wait to get my hands on that crown," she said. "Are you sad about giving it up?"

Reese shook her head. "Only a little. I mean, it's been a great year, and you're going to enjoy every minute of it I'm sure, but I think I'm about ready to be done with it and move on. You know?"

The girl reached into her makeup bag before twisting a small lid off a tube of lip gloss. She smothered it over her top lip as she spoke. "I don't know," she said, moving to the bottom lip. "I'm not gonna stop here. I plan to go onto Brazoria County, Miss Texas, Miss America. I want it all."

Reese smiled, charmed by the young woman's ambition.

There was quite a difference in their ages. Pearland's new rose had won at the young age of eighteen, while Reese had taken the crown at the maximum age of twenty-three. "Well, good for you. I'll be cheering ya on from the sidelines," she said before closing the stall door. The latch to lock the metal door was old and rusty. Nearly impossible to slide. She tightened her grip around the dull knob and shoved, the loud 'pop' filling the quiet space. "Sorry," Reese said. "Stubborn lock."

Her gaze fell to the small tiles on the floor as she folded her arms over her chest, wishing she could skip the ceremony altogether, slip out the back door and go home. Her interaction with the man on the dance floor had her feeling nervous. Afraid, though she knew it was foolish. The guy couldn't possibly mean her harm. He'd only been awkward was all. Not dangerous. She nodded to herself, convinced to shake it off.

With a wave of assurance urging her forward, Reese reached for the latch to unlock the stall. Just as she shoved the stubborn thing into place, an ear-splitting explosion rocked the room. Reese pressed her hands to her ears and ducked down, cringing as the deafening blast echoed throughout the small space.

A gunshot? Had somebody just shot a gun? Her heart thudded against her chest, the pressing rhythm making it hard to breathe. A sharp ringing pierced her ears as she lifted her chin, and then straightened to a stand altogether. Through the crack of the stall frame, a view of the mirror came into sight. Only she didn't see the girl. Instead Reese saw a man reflected there – his green eyes wild. And then he was gone, lost in the black fabric folds.

The door creaked to a close. The shrill ringing only intensified as she yanked open the flimsy stall door. Blood. A dark, oozing pool of it soaked the satin banner across the young girl's chest. A hand flew to Reese's mouth as she screamed, a horrid realization coming to mind: The man in the mirror – it had been him. The one who'd sent her rushing to the restroom in fear. He was dangerous after all. And though it hurt to think it, Reese was certain the bullet in the girl's chest had been meant for her.

This ends the sample of Reese's Cowboy Kiss. To continue reading, pick up your copy here.

FREE BOOK

Subscribe to my newsletter and receive my novella, Ranch Hand for Auction, FREE as a thank you gift!

ALSO BY KIMBERLY KREY

Unlikely Cowgirl Series

Once Hitched Twice Shy

How to Catch a Cowboy in 10 Days

This Cowboy's a Keeper

Cobble Creek Small Town Romance

The Unlikely Bride

The Hopeful Bride

The Determined Bride

The Sweet Montana Bride Series

Reese's Cowboy Kiss

Jade's Cowboy Crush

Cassie's Cowboy Crave

Second Chances Series

Rough Edges

Mending Herats

Fresh Starts

Beach Romance

Catching Waves: A Sweet Beach Romance (The Royal Palm Resort Book 2)

Young Adult Novellas

Getting Kole for Christmas

Getting Micah under the Mistletoe

Chemistry of a Kiss

Novella

Ranch Hand for Auction

Navy SEALs Romance

The Honorable Warrior

The Fearless Warrior

Also see

Her TV Bachelor Fake Fiancé

The Cowboy's Catch (in Big Sky Anthology)

ABOUT THE AUTHOR

Writing Romance That's Clean Without Losing the Steam!

Award-winning author Kimberly Krey has always been a fan of good, clean romance, so she decided to specialize in writing 'Romance That's Clean without Losing the Steam'. She's a fervent lover of God, family, and cheese platters, as well as the ultimate hater of laundry. Follow her on any of the sites below for updates on new releases and or giveaways.

facebook.com/kimberlykreyauthor
twitter.com/KimberlyKrey
instagram.com/romance_is_write
bookbub.com/profile/kimberly-krey

www.ingramcontent.com/pod-product-compliance
Ingram Content Group UK Ltd.
Pitfield, Milton Keynes, MK11 3LW, UK
UKHW012254290726
14090UKWH00016B/635

9 781079 972313